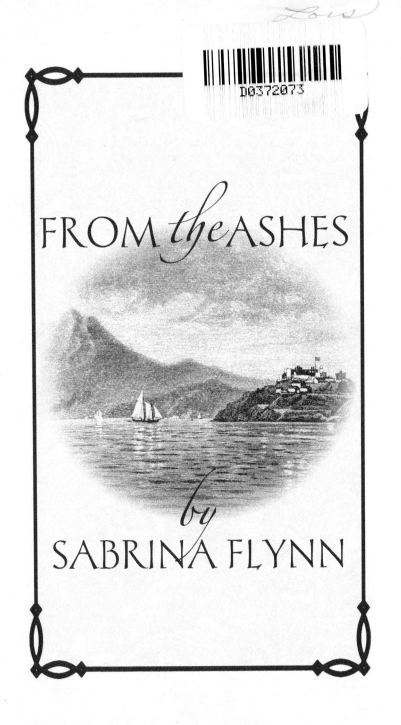

FROM *the* ASHES

by SABRINA FLYNN

for Ben
my own Riot

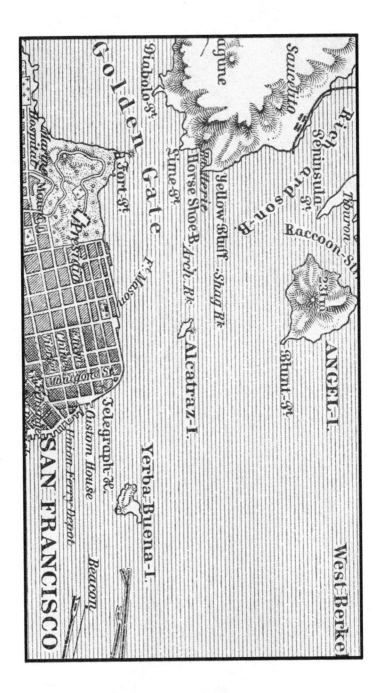

Preface

THE BONE ORCHARD WAS silent. As were the two men standing on top of memories. The younger of the two was worn, pale, and hatless. A bandage wrapped around his temples. He leaned heavily on his silver-knobbed stick while an older man with a bushy white beard rocked back and forth on his heels.

"It's a real nice gravesite, A.J. Just up the hill there."

The younger did not respond.

"You were like a son to Zeph—the closest he could have had, anyhow. Left you everything, including the agency. Things will get right, you'll see."

"Ravenwood should be here, not me."

"Zeph would likely say somethin' about your fanciful wishing."

The younger man frowned. After a time, he murmured, "He already did."

The older man fixed a worried gaze on his friend. "Well, if you don't intend to say goodbye, we best get you home. Some rest will put you right."

"I'm not going home, Tim. I can't face his empty chair." The younger man touched the bandage over his right temple and closed his eyes. The bone orchard fell away. Blood and death and failure exploded behind his eyes. Around and around—a revolving vision.

Ashes to ashes; dust to dust. Unfortunately, memories weren't so easily buried.

1

A Gentleman Returns

UNKNOWINGLY HE ARRIVED WITH the plague. It was fitting, divine almost, for he had left with death on his heels, and now he was bringing an old companion home.

The pair had sailed into port on a four-masted steamer, the S.S. *Australia*. It now towered alongside the wharf, spewing passengers down its gangplank. The ramp bowed under their eager weight. Boots thudded on planks, voices clamored, and a surge of porters rushed forward to stake their claim on weary travelers.

A single gentleman stopped at the gangplank's end. He was not a tall man, nor a large one, but he was steady and unwavering and the tide of humanity flowed around his presence.

Atticus James Riot stared at the tips of his polished shoes. With methodical indifference to the glares directed at his back, he set down his Gladstone, removed his round spectacles, polished the glass with silk, and resettled the wire on his nose. Through an unblemished sheen, he scanned the docks.

They surged with chaos. Harried dockworkers swarmed over the steamers and wharves like an army of ants, unloading and loading goods into waiting wagons.

Seeking comfort, he raised his eyes to the city, to familiar hills and rising spires. His heart soared, but only for a moment. The sweetness of home left an aftertaste of bitterness and grief. Resigned, he took a breath, placed his stick on the dock and stepped forward, arriving in San Francisco, a city he had once known intimately.

California's Silver Mistress greeted him with a lush, sensuous embrace. She was a late riser who generally left at noon, returning in the evening like a slow crashing wave rolling relentlessly towards the port. Her touch was cool and it settled around his bones. He had missed her caress.

Turning his nose to the mist, he breathed her in, flipped up his collar, and waded into his old hunting grounds.

The crowds flowed towards a clock tower to the north. Contrary to their rushing strides, he moved at a leisurely pace, circling a family of Italian immigrants. The infant bawled, the children squealed, and the parents looked lost and mystified all at once. He tipped his hat to the woman, and silently wished the family good luck.

Dreams only carried one so far in this city.

Riot had been abroad three years, and in his absence an ornate building had replaced the old wooden gateway to San Francisco's ferry terminals. Its tower, still caged in scaffolding, rose over a bristling bay of masts. Thunder rolled from its base where four tracks converged at the foot of Market.

Travelers poured on and off cable cars. Bells, horns, shouts, and a tumult of rattling hacks mingled with the earthshaking noise. He stopped beside a lamp post, and leaned casually on his silver-knobbed stick, watching travelers argue over hacks and pile into cable cars, eager to escape the chaos.

Everyone had somewhere to be, except Riot. He was in no particular hurry to finish his journey. Home beckoned, but not with hope or promise.

However, the fates conspired, hurling a perceptive hackman in front of the well-dressed gentleman.

The cabriolet rolled to a stop in front of Riot. A nag that looked more donkey than horse nipped at his pinstriped trousers, and the driver, who resembled his horse, bared his remaining teeth.

"Well, if it isn't the detective who shanghaied himself," the hackman crowed around the stem of his pipe. "Finally found your way back to port, A.J."

"Only to fall into the hands of the very crimper who sent me far from shore." The hackman, in cap and peacoat, was certainly dressed like a seaman.

"If only I was so smart. Well, don't stand there; climb in before I'm hijacked."

Riot eyed the deranged old man, whose bushy white beard resembled that of a crazed St. Nick. He ran a hand over his trimmed beard, as if mere proximity to the wild mass would taint his own.

"How is it, Tim, that I'm gone for three years, yet within an hour of returning you find me?"

"Call it a knack. Might say a speciality."

"More likely a greased palm at the custom station." Riot handed his Gladstone up, tucked his stick under his arm, and settled on the seat next to Tim. "You've taken up hack driving in your spare time?"

"That's right," Tim snorted, urging the horse forward. The cab lurched, bumping over the uneven street. "I retired from crimping after throwing you to the dogs. You ready to get back in the investigating business, then?"

"I'm retired, Tim."

"You're too young to retire."

"Hardly," Riot drawled. "Didn't you notice the grey in my beard, or have your eyes failed in my absence?"

"My one good eye is better than the two of yours."

"More reason to retire."

Tim glanced to the side, appraising his passenger, who appeared as agile as the boy who had once tried to pick his pocket. "You can't be a day over forty if you remember at all."

"Forty-three, or thereabouts, by my estimation."

"Never took you for a man who'd dig his grave early."

"I would sleep easier if it were only my own," Riot replied, severely.

"Gawd dammit," Tim swore, but whether it was directed at the hay wagon and cable car that were hogging the road, or at Riot, was not immediately apparent. With an expert hand, Tim maneuvered his cab around the lumbering wagon, dodged an oncoming motorcar, and swerved in front of the cable car. A bicyclist turned sharply towards the curb and the pedestrians, left to fend for themselves, bolted like startled hens. "Put it in the past, A.J. It's been three years. Ravenwood is good and buried."

Riot sighed, closing his eyes to a vision of terror and blood.

"Besides," Tim persisted, "an apprentice isn't allowed to retire before his teacher."

"Teacher?" Riot pushed up the brim of his fedora, staring at the older man in amusement. "The only things I recall you ever teaching me is everything I'd never admit to knowing."

"You knew them well enough before I got a hold of you," Tim retorted. "Besides, a teacher's a teacher."

"One more profession to add to your prodigious list."

"And still growing," Tim said with pride. "Not much left to me except harlotry."

The younger man winced. "I hope to be long dead before that happens."

"Unless you plan on dying soon, you won't miss it. I've been saving that trade for my eightieth birthday."

"I'm fairly certain I don't want to know your reasoning behind that scheme."

"Plan on charging a dollar per year. I reckon you can't put a price on experience."

"Certainly not on that kind," Riot agreed dryly.

"Your faith in me is heartening." Tim turned down Post towards Franklin, and calmer roads. "Look here, I've got a job tailor-made for you."

"You're more than able, Tim."

"I need help."

"You have other investigators."

"With heads full of bricks. Smith and Johnson do a fair job, but this case calls for a certain amount of refinement and delicacy. The agency hasn't been the same without you."

Riot looked at the small man with the wild white beard. Tim had always looked more like a mad leprechaun than a detective. "I never asked you to manage the agency."

"Ravenwood spent his life building that agency. I'll not let it die because his partner got the jitters."

The air turned cold in Riot's lungs. He squeezed the knob of his walking stick until his knuckles turned white. "Direct your client to Pinkerton's," he said, tersely.

"If *my* client hired Pinkerton's men, there'd be a riot. What with the anti-Pinkerton Act and all. Besides, he wants the best and you're the best. Just so happens he'll get a Riot after all."

"I see your puns haven't suffered in my absence."

"My knees have. I need a young'un for the rough work."

"I thought you required refinement and delicacy?"

"Both attributes of a sharp blade."

"If the client can't hire Pinkerton's men, it means he's either a politician or in the same boat with them. You know how I feel about that sort." Ironically, the cabriolet was bouncing through an affluent neighborhood filled with those very people: San Francisco's puppeteers, who made the city dance to their whims.

"So you're going to make the young lady who was abducted suffer for your prejudice?"

Riot pressed his lips together. Tim always knew how to reel him in.

"It's a puzzle, just the kind you like, with a damsel in distress to boot. How can you resist?"

"By resisting," Riot stated.

"But you're not allowed. One last case, that's all I'm asking," pleaded Tim. "Think of it as a favor for an old friend."

"A favor?"

"Might be your last chance."

Riot glanced at Tim, and then away, letting his gaze rove over the ornate houses and their slim turrets. He didn't much care for Tim's use of words: 'old' and 'last' were permanent.

"Begging is beneath you."

"Well, I can't twist your arm like I used to." Tim tossed Riot the reins and plucked his pipe from between his lips to relight it.

"Particulars of the case?"

"I'm not saying a word until you agree," Tim huffed, knocking his pipe against his palm. Ashes fluttered to the cobblestones.

"I'm going to need more bait than that."

"I'll give you three words, and that's all."

Riot inclined his head.

"Two ransom demands."

"Two?" Riot narrowed his eyes. "How far apart?"

"Not a word more till you agree." The nag snorted, reinforcing Tim's ultimatum.

One more case in San Francisco, but without his mentor and partner—the brilliant half of the agency. Riot had solved his fair share of cases, but his last blunder was unforgivable. He nudged the brim of his fedora up, and rubbed at his temple, where a streak of white slashed across his raven hair.

"Fine," he relented at length, "but I'm retiring after this final case."

"And I'm a crimper," Tim muttered, taking the reins.

"Pardon me?"

"I said, how was Honolulu?"

"Like a kettle about to explode."

"India?"

"Hot."

"And Paris?"

"Hot."

"How 'bout the women?"

Riot primly adjusted his spectacles. "Mind the carriage, Tim."

The old man cackled. "By the way, I should warn you that after you left me in charge of Ravenwood's place—your estate now—I might have rented it out to a few boarders."

"I'm surprised you didn't open a parlor house."

"Only one room," Tim admitted.

Riot closed his eyes and ran a hand over his beard. It was, he reflected, not too late to turn coward and fall back into his nomadic ways.

2

An Uneasy Welcome

THE HOUSE WAS AS imposing as Riot remembered. Sitting arrogantly on its hill, peaked roofs, curving iron and rounded turrets. A brooding matriarch presiding over the city with disdain, much as her previous owner had. The late Zephaniah Ravenwood would have grumbled at the light spilling from the windows. They shone like a lighthouse beacon, warmth seeping through curtains with merry welcome. Judging from the number of lights, it looked as though every room in the house was occupied.

Despite the surprising transformation, a shadow lay over the house, or so Riot fancied. He pulled his long coat closer, warding against a sudden chill. "A hotel would suit me just fine, Tim," Riot said abruptly.

"A hotel?" Tim looked at Riot as if he'd sprouted wings. "Why the devil would you waste cash on that when you have a perfectly good home?"

"Inhabited by strangers," he pointed out. "Besides, it looks full to bursting, and I wouldn't want to put your boarders out."

Tim drove the carriage into a narrow lane alongside the house, and clucked the nag to a halt. When the cabriolet settled, Tim hopped down, staring up at the reluctant arrival with knowing blue eyes.

"You haven't set foot in this house since Zeph was murdered. Don't you think it's high time you buried that hatchet?"

Riot winced at the choice of words. He shoved memory aside, and frowned down at the wizened old man. "Ravenwood hated it when you called him that."

"I know." Tim grinned, retrieving his bag.

Against his will, Riot stepped down. The urge to turn tail and play the coward was a bitter taste in his mouth. With an air of finality, Tim shoved the Gladstone into his arms. It was decided; he'd face his demons square. There was no turning back.

"No one's in the turret room. I left it as it was, and kept it locked."

The load suddenly lightened in his hand. He glanced down to find a small dark-skinned boy at his side, attempting to lift his bag.

"I can carry that for you, sir."

"That there's Tobias," Tim introduced, and then nodded towards the tall lad who was taking charge of the horse. "And his brother, Grimm."

Impressed by the lads' light feet, Riot touched his hat in greeting and surrendered his Gladstone. Tobias stumbled under the bag's weight, but persevered, dragging it towards the grocer's entrance.

"Grimm?" Riot inquired.

"Ain't never smiled," Tim grunted. "More I think on it, the name would suit you."

"I know how you hate a missed opportunity."

"Tobias, take that up to the turret room." Tobias and Grimm froze.

"The turret?" the smaller boy asked.

"I'll be up to unlock it," Tim explained. Both boys looked from Tim to Riot, and stared, their mouths gaping. There was fear in their eyes. Here was the man who could throw them all out on the street.

The master of the house has arrived, thought Riot, without assurances and fully intending to rid himself of Ravenwood's estate. Nothing, he reflected, was ever straightforward, especially when Tim was involved.

Grimm recovered first, returning quietly to his work of unhitching the horse, while a jolt of energy hit the smaller brother, propelling him forward. The Gladstone bumped its way into the house.

"Ma," the boy shouted, "the turret room man is here to kick us all out."

Riot grimaced, removing his hat and gloves in one smooth sweep. Smells of fresh bread and stew and everything welcoming greeted him, followed by a woman whose skin was as rich as coffee. Her dark eyes were as warm, but as with any strong cup, there was complexity in the depths. Resignation swirled to the surface.

Tim turned bright as a brick, tripping over his words. "Real pleasure to see you, Miss Lily. This is, that is, may I introduce Atticus Riot."

"Everyone calls me Miss Lily."

"A pleasure," Riot inclined his head. "You keep a fine house, Miss Lily."

"I keep it as I would my own, nothing more. A house needs some care, Mr. Riot, or it falls apart. We'll make what arrangements you like and if you'll be staying I'll have my sons move the occupant from the big room for you."

"No need," Riot hastened. "The turret will suit me just fine."

Miss Lily smoothed her immaculate apron and steeled herself with a breath. "May I ask, Mr. Riot, if you'll want us gone? I'd like to let the boarders know soon as possible."

Riot swept a dark, appraising gaze over the hallway and kitchen. The counters gleamed, the wood floors were worn but polished, the papered walls and paneling thrived in the light, and the hum of conversation drifted from the common rooms.

"I have no plans as of yet, Miss Lily, but whatever I decide, I'll give ample notice."

Miss Lily nodded. "Supper is ready at eight every evening. Nothing formal, mind you. The boarders serve themselves in the dining room—"

"I won't be joining the others," Riot interrupted, hoarsely. The walls closed in, his hand trembled ever so slightly, and he gripped the knob of his stick, unable to apologize for his rudeness. Miss Lily's eyes went wide with surprise.

Tim cleared his throat. "He likes to eat alone. Maybe Maddie can bring up a tray."

"Yes," Riot recovered. "That'd be preferable."

Miss Lily studied the new master of the house with equal parts worry and puzzlement before nodding in reply.

Tim shifted from foot to foot. "Smells like heaven, Miss Lily, as always."

"If it's heaven you're after, then you'll need to clean up,

or you won't be passing those pearly gates to the feast."

"Well worth the effort, ma'am."

"And you always need a lot of that, Mr. Tim," Miss Lily laughed, sweet and melodious. "You'd best get started."

"Yes, ma'am."

As Lily sauntered back into her domain, Riot arched a brow at his flustered companion.

"Shut it, boy," Tim scowled, springing towards the servant's stairway in retreat. Riot followed, taking the stairs slowly, dreading what he would find at the top.

3

Two Empty Chairs

"ARE YOU ALL RIGHT, A.J.?" A voice drifted in the dark room.

"I believe I indicated my preference for a hotel," Riot returned, navigating the darkness. Avoiding the greater shadows, he twined his way through the clutter towards the windows while Tim fiddled with the gas lamps.

"The house has been scrubbed from top to bottom and back up again. You'll find nothing but life."

"And plenty of memories."

A soft light suffused the circular room, illuminating its ghostly contents. Riot turned from the brightness, avoided the two chairs by the cold hearth, and nudged a curtain aside to gaze at a fitful fog instead.

Tim eyed the detective. The years had weathered Riot's exuberance, worn away the rough edges and left him hard. Veins of steel ran through his short beard and a mark of wisdom slashed across his temple.

Tim rocked back on his heels and returned to his toes. "Plenty of time left to make new ones."

"Leave it, Tim," Riot warned. A shadow stirred the fog. The disturbance strode through the gardens with a confident swagger. "I see our resident lady of the night entertains her clients in Ravenwood's old consultation room."

"How'd you guess?"

"I should think the French doors make an ideal room for liaisons."

"Annie is real respectable," Tim defended.

"How I've missed San Francisco and her society," Riot mused, letting the curtain fall back in place. "One of the few places where you'll hear 'respectable' applied to a prostitute."

"Oldest profession there is," Tim shrugged. "Never understood all the fuss. Scarce as women were in forty-nine, the ground was sacred where a woman walked—any woman."

"Straightforward, as always." The edge of Riot's lip quirked. "I do believe I have missed you."

"It happens," Tim sniffed, wiping his nose on his sleeve. "Not the same since you left."

Riot glanced at the two pieces of draped furniture by the fireplace. He knew those worn chairs by heart, could see them in his mind's eye along with every book that used to fill now-barren shelves. Despite his weariness, he could not bring himself to sit in his old chair and stare at the emptiness across. Instead, he walked over to something resembling a hat stand, pulled off the drape, and hung his fedora and coat on a hook. "Did you bring your case notes?"

"Don't you want to eat or—" Tim gestured vaguely around the room. "Settle in?"

"I would like to retire," Riot said, sitting on the edge of a crate near the window. "The sooner this case is complete, the sooner I may do so." Deep brown eyes that were nearly black in the subdued light settled on Tim expectantly.

In answer, Tim patted his coat, trousers, and waistcoat, muttering under his breath until he pulled a tattered notepad from beneath his belt. The spry older man situated himself in front of the fireplace. He held the notepad aloft, at arm's length, and cleared his throat as if preparing to deliver an oration. Squinting appeared to help him decipher the scrawl.

"On Tuesday, December 26th, shortly after her husband left for Oakland, Isobel Kingston told the staff that she intended to visit her family in Sausalito. She took a hack from her home on Nob Hill. The fare was paid to Market, but the hackman said she exited just short of the ferry building. The intersection was jammed by an accident. The hackman thought she was in a hurry.

"Of all the travelers, ferry crew, ticket counters, and dockhands we questioned, Smith managed to find two witnesses, a mother and daughter by the name of Worth, who placed her on the 9:00 ferry. None of the other passengers could confirm or deny this. Mrs. Kingston never arrived at her family's home. And no one realized she was missing until the next morning when her father, Marcus Amsel, received a ransom demand."

Riot crossed his arms. "Her family wasn't aware she would be visiting?"

"They were not," Tim replied. "She wanted to spend Christmas with her family, but had canceled due to her husband's plans. The day she was abducted, Mr. Kingston left at 6:45 on an urgent matter: one of his warehouses had been targeted by an arsonist. According to the household staff, Mrs. Kingston left very shortly after her husband, telling the staff she would visit her family, but she didn't send word ahead to the family."

"Are we speaking of *the* Alex Kingston? Attorney to San Francisco's elite?"

Tim nodded. "The very one. Property investor and lawyer. He's a wealthy man in his own right."

"And what of Mrs. Kingston's father?"

"Marcus Amsel is a wine merchant and his wife hails from a family of boat builders. After Mrs. Amsel's parents died, she inherited the family business. Her husband runs the enterprise now, along with three of his eight remaining sons."

Riot arched a brow. "How many daughters?"

"Just one on this side of the veil," replied Tim. "And it seems the boatbuilding business has taken some hard knocks in the last year. Lost the family a lot of money."

"Odd then, that the ransom demand would be sent to the father and not the wealthy husband," Riot mused. "What were the demands?"

"One hundred thousand cash, stuffed in a black bag, placed in a rowboat, and tied to the end of a long wharf at Mr. Amsel's shipyards. They gave him a week to gather the money. If the police are brought in, then she'll be killed, but things became a bit complicated when another demand appeared on the front pages of the *Sunday Call*, *Chronicle*, and *Bulletin*."

"The front page?" Riot asked in surprise, rubbing his chin.

"I know, it don't make much sense. Back in a lick."

Tim darted from the room with the nimbleness of an old billy goat.

Riot pondered the ceiling for an exasperated moment before drifting slowly over to the two armchairs. He ran his fingers over a drape, gently tugging it free to reveal a stately chair that could double as a throne.

Zephaniah Ravenwood had loathed comfort. A relaxed body, he often intoned, impeded one's mental faculties.

A movement by the door caught Riot's eye. The outline of a small shadow spread over the hardwood floors.

"You may as well come in, Tobias." Riot's offer was answered by a squeak.

The boy shuffled inside, looking shamefaced and nervous.

"I hold no tolerance for eavesdropping, young man," Riot reproved, and then softened, "Unless it's done properly. How much did you overhear?"

The boy shyly summarized the entire conversation.

"A woman's life is at stake," Riot said, firmly. "Not a word of this to anyone. Do you understand?"

"Yes, sir."

"Will you swear yourself to secrecy?"

"I will, sir."

"Good, sit down, and if you have anything to add, then do so." Riot gestured towards his dead partner's chair. Tobias sat, eyes wide and roving.

Ravenwood's presence lingered in the room, settling heavily on Riot's shoulders. But as long as the boy remained in the chair, that presence was tolerable. And it amused Riot that his partner would have had an apoplectic fit to see a boy in his chair.

Shortly, Tim returned with newspapers in hand. He

blinked at Tobias, glanced at Riot, and chuckled before handing the papers over.

Riot spread three newspapers along with one hand-written note on the crate. The note was nearly illegible, riddled with poor grammar, spelling, and punctuation: *'You wil have to pay us before you git her from us, and pay us a big cent to if you put the cops hunting for her you is only defeegin yu own end.'* The note continued, detailing pick up time and location, which was odd in itself. Usually, the criminals sent a second note, closer to the exchange date.

"It's a poor job," Riot murmured. Tobias appeared between the two, standing on his toes to peer at the papers. "Notice they can spell 'hunting' perfectly well, but not 'get' and 'will'. I'll wager the wharf was carefully chosen too. No nearby coves or inlets to hide in?" Tim nodded. "I thought so. I see they've picked an hour when the fog will be thick."

"Correct on all accounts," Tim confirmed.

"They're locals, no doubt about that." Riot sniffed at the crudely penned note. "Too many hands," he muttered, nonsensically, as if answering a question, "but the paper is coarser than it should be, stiffer. You'll notice the slant and unevenness to the hand and unsteadiness of the lines. This was written on rough wood, not a desk, but the unevenness isn't drastic enough for a carriage or train. And see here, the ink spread and didn't take in places."

"Salt."

"This was penned on a boat. Our abductors are definitely watermen, or working with someone who is. How was the note delivered?"

"A local gin enthusiast. She goes by the name of Old Sue. Always loitering down by the docks looking for a—" Tim glanced at Tobias and altered his choice of words, "desperate client. She was paid a total sum of two bottles to deliver the note."

"Did she remember anything?"

"After two bottles? No."

"Did you have one of your boys sober her up?"

"Old Sue hasn't been sober for twenty years," Tim grunted. "It would likely kill her. I checked back with her a few days ago. Didn't recall anything more."

Riot frowned, nudged the note aside, and turned his scrutiny to the newspapers. The headlines were bold and simple, aimed at Alex Kingston and followed by an exposé that mentioned every dime novel plot ever conceived, from Tongs to White Slavery:

TYCOON'S BRIDE ABDUCTED!
RANSOM DEMANDED
"WE HAVE YOUR WIFE, KINGSTON. GATHER YOUR WEALTH
FOR HER SAFE RETURN."

"The same letter was sent to all three newspapers," Tim explained. "They arrived by mail, stamped with a San Francisco mark. Course the police are all over this case now. Since it looks like some Chinaman set fire to Kingston's warehouse in Oakland, they've been tearing apart Chinatown and using the ransom as an excuse to board every junk in the bay."

"Has Kingston received a private letter detailing their demands?"

"Not yet," Tim said, scratching his bald pate. "I'm not too proud to admit that this has me stumped. My boys haven't turned up so much as a whisper, and the press and police are dredging up a mess."

"It's quite a pretty little problem, as the Great Detective would say."

"Don't know about pretty, but sure enough it's a pile of

horse shit."

"The style and method of the two demands differs greatly. I think we're dealing with two separate sets of criminals. Obviously, the first wants money, but again, why demand ransom from the father when the husband is wealthier? And the second——"

"Wants everyone and his mother to know that Mrs. Kingston is in jeopardy," Tim inserted.

"Precisely," Riot agreed. "I believe the second is personal. A jab at Alex Kingston."

"But which group has her?" Tim asked, scratching his nose. "And since the whole city knows, will the first have already killed her?"

"I'm sure you've been digging into both Kingston's and Amsel's affairs. Have you found any obvious enemies?"

"Kingston can count half the city as an enemy. As far as Amsel is concerned, he's as honest a businessman as you can find. He and his family are well thought of in Sausalito. You can look over my notes on the interview. Since I don't exactly fit the detective image that Kingston had in mind, I've had a fellow by the name of Matthew Smith handling his questioning. Smith is an ex-patrolman. Couldn't tolerate the corruption. So you don't think this is a common gang?"

"If it weren't for the newspaper announcement, then I'd suspect the mundane, but this second demand hints at something more."

"I've been thinking that there might have been a disagreement between the abductors, and a few of them splintered off, taking the girl."

"Most hoodlums would wait until after payment was received."

"Maybe, maybe not, but not much else makes sense."

"Did Amsel tell anyone about the first ransom demand?"

"He sent one of his sons, Curtis, to tell Kingston. And then Kingston personally contacted Ravenwood Agency— against Amsel's wishes."

"The father was going to pay the money and hope for the best?"

"That he was," Tim nodded. "Kingston refuses to budge on the ransom payment. Him and Amsel had a proper row. He's convinced they'll kill her whether or not the payment is received, so he hired us to look for her discreetly while Amsel is selling off his assets to fill a bag with cash. Course, once the newspaper headlines appeared, Kingston got his back up and hollered something fierce. Poor Smith is too terrified to talk to the man again."

"Kingston is right," Riot sighed. "In all likelihood they will kill her, especially if there's been some sort of disagreement." He frowned at the newspapers. "The second demand is curious. The letters sent to the newspapers weren't handwritten; the article says that the words were cut from older editions and pasted on the note paper. Not many criminals are worried about handwriting recognition, or even realize it's possible. The author in the first demand wasn't overly concerned with such details, while the second demand borders on paranoia. Clearly, our newspaper letters were sent by someone who was not only worried that his hand writing would be recognized, but someone familiar with a detective's methods."

"Sherlock Holmes does it all the time, sir," Tobias offered.

"Excellent point, Tobias," Riot nodded to the boy. "Our letter writer could very well be a fanciful amateur with a taste for dime novels. What do we know about Mrs. Kingston besides the newspaper's flowery drivel describing her as a 'fair-haired, wilting feminine flower of San Francisco society' whose honor is in grave danger?"

"Kingston described his wife as a 'delicate' young woman of twenty."

"Delicate in constitution or build?"

Tim flipped through his notes, scowling at the offending paper. "Smith didn't ask for specifics."

"He should have."

"Well, like I said, his head is full of bricks," Tim grumbled. "It's not easy finding a good detective, but he has a face to please the gentry. Besides, I wouldn't have thought to question Kingston about his wife's bust and hip measurements, either."

"Surely you have some experience as a tailor?"

"I do, but I dealt with men folk," Tim explained primly. "Now look here." He jabbed a finger at his notes. "Mr. Amsel put her at a pinch over five feet, and described his daughter as an 'outdoors enthusiast', so I reckon Kingston was referring to her height."

"Since you're shorter, would that make you even more delicate?"

"Maybe so, but then you'd only be slightly less delicate. And I've never had no complaints about my stature," Tim returned.

"How long have the Kingstons been married? As I recall, Kingston isn't a young man."

"Two months," Tim replied. "There was a big 'to do' in the papers. Mrs. Kingston was attending the University of California."

"How many years?" Riot inquired.

"She enrolled last September. Was studying Law."

"And quit after two months to marry Kingston?"

"Well, it *was* Law," Tim shrugged. "You know how these society ladies are—fluttering here and there, changing their minds on a whim."

"Society ladies don't generally enroll at university. Had they known each other long?"

"According to the gossips, no," Tim replied. "They met over the summer at a dinner party."

"Seems rushed to me."

"I suppose it does," Tim admitted. "Might make sense if he were a good-looking fellow. Women get all airy over a pretty face, but Kingston's older than you and double the man."

"Age and girth are secondary to wealth."

"Maybe so, but he also has the disposition of a bull."

"I'm told diamonds are the primary cause of blindness in women," Riot observed.

"I suppose there's no hope of you retiring and finding a good woman?"

"Cynicism is all the comfort I require."

"Didn't used to be," Tim muttered.

"Not to worry, I'm not chock-full of stinging wind yet. There's far too much doom and gloom in me, and as such, I think we ought to poke into the Kingstons' marriage a bit more."

"I'll see what I can dig up."

"Now, let's focus on her disappearance. It was the day after Christmas, when most folks return home or visit friends, so very likely the ferry was crowded."

Tim nodded in confirmation.

"On the ferry, what drew the mother's and daughter's attention to Mrs. Kingston?"

"The Worths admired the color of her hair and eyes.

Like spun gold and amber they said. She was, they said, very fashionably attired in a green hat and walking dress trimmed in gold, although they thought her long coat was a poor choice."

"And what was unfortunate about her choice of a coat?"

"It was 'dreary', they said."

"Dreary as in the color, condition, cut, or all of the above?"

"Er—" Tim stammered, shifting from foot to foot as his ears turned pink. "Well, it was dark, the color that is."

"Black, grey, blue, puce?"

"I didn't think much of it, so I didn't ask," he admitted in defeat.

"Did our unperceptive duo note anything else?"

"They thought her 'most rude' for a young woman." Tim pitched his voice to surprising heights: "*She had no inclination to engage us in conversation.*"

"Was she carrying luggage?"

"A 'faded green and beige leafy carpet bag'."

"That's rather troubling," Riot murmured, gazing at the newspapers in thought.

"What?"

"All of it, most especially her 'dreary long coat'."

"How so?"

"That remains to be seen."

"Is that another damn quote?"

"You should read more."

"I do read. Practical things like newspapers," Tim retorted. "Not those dime novels you fill your head with."

"If you bothered to read them, then you would know that detectives never stray from the point."

Riot placed his hands on either side of the crate, and

bent to examine a newspaper article bearing a photograph of Mrs. Isobel Kingston. It was hard to determine if she was handsome or not—certainly not in a classical sense, but without a doubt, she was striking. Her eyes were half averted, her lips pressed together in a hard, determined line. She reminded him of a cornered tigress, both fearful and fierce, on the verge of leaping.

"The point being?" Tim pressed.

"*All action is of the mind,*" Riot said softly, "*and the mirror of the mind is the face, its index the eyes.*" He abruptly straightened, and gathered his coat and hat.

"Where you off to?"

"To learn what I can," Riot said, slipping on his gloves. "Is Kingston still a member of the Pacific-Union Club?"

"As is every other businessman in San Francisco," Tim grunted, handing Riot the case notes. "I'll get the hack then."

"No need, Tim. I've been trapped on a steamer for a solid month; the walk will do me good." Riot paused in the doorway. "What's the earliest ferry to Sausalito?"

"7:30."

Riot blinked, and tilted his head, as if listening to a distant noise. "And the next one?"

"9:00."

"You said Alex Kingston left at 6:45, and his wife left shortly after. What ferry did the Worths spot her on?"

"The 9:00."

"And no one noticed her in the ferry building?"

"Not that I can find."

"Mr. Tobias," Riot looked at the boy. "Can your brother Grimm handle the cabriolet?"

"Yes, sir."

"Can you read a watch?"

"Yes, sir."

Riot unhooked his silver chain from its eyehole, and deposited watch and chain in the boy's hand. "I'd like you both to conduct an experiment for me tomorrow. First thing in the morning, around 7:00, time how long it takes you to drive from Alex Kingston's home on Nob Hill to the ferry building."

"Sure thing, Mr. Riot."

"Mind the watch." Riot squeezed the boy's shoulder and addressed Tim. "If I don't return tonight, I'll meet you on the boat."

As Riot's footsteps faded rapidly down the winding stairway, Tim grinned at Tobias, "And he thinks he's retiring."

4

The Husband

THE CABLE CAR WAS dragged up an impossible road. At the
hill's peak, Riot stepped off the running board, dodged a
pair of weary horses, and climbed the steps to a sprawling
brownstone. Bright bulbs of electric light guided his easy
ascent. The glass doors opened, welcoming his gender and
attire.

Riot's footsteps echoed in the entranceway. He removed his hat and gloves, passing them off to a severe
attendant.

"I'm a guest of Alex Kingston." Riot presented his
card. "Kindly inform him of my arrival."

"If you will wait in the French room." With a whispered word, the attendant passed the card to another man
of paleness and jet, and then swept his arm towards a side
door. Riot was shown from the hall of echoing splendor to

a smaller room of dark wood and leather. He settled himself in a comfortable chair before a window, waved away the offered cigar and brandy, and patiently waited.

The Pacific Union Club dominated Nob Hill while the rest of the world knelt at its feet. Fog crept along the wide windows, muting the city's lights. They were like tiny lanterns adrift in a dark swirling sea.

Time ticked, the pendulum swung in its gilded embrace, and the Grandfather rang ten, a mournful sound that heralded an imposing presence. Heavy footsteps marched across wood and Riot rose, turning to meet his client for the first time.

"Has your damn agency found my wife yet?" Alex Kingston filled the room like a statue in a square. Well into his fifties, as solid as an ox, and severe as stone.

"If that were the case, a telegram would have sufficed," Riot answered easily.

Kingston stopped directly in front, looming over the smaller man. Riot raised his eyes from a broad expanse of starched shirtfront to Kingston's face. The man's eyes were pale and icy, and his nose broad and flat.

"I want my wife returned," Kingston rumbled as if addressing her abductor.

Riot stood his ground, forcing the larger man to take a step back. "Of course you do," he answered, "or you wouldn't have contracted our agency's services."

To hide his failed gamble, Kingston turned towards the sideboard. "You haven't found her."

"No, but I do have questions that may aid our investigation."

"I already answered your associate's questions. What was his name—Smith."

"Your wife is missing, Mr. Kingston," Riot said, resuming his seat. "Is there a limit to the number of questions you're willing to answer?"

The large man sighed, swirling his brandy thoughtfully. After a moment, he downed the snifter in one gulp.

"No, of course not." His shoulders deflated and he sat heavily in the chair opposite. "The thought of her with those men—a man can only take so much." Kingston gripped the armrest, knuckles white and straining.

Riot feared for the armrest's future.

"I have some questions that want answering and then I'll leave you to your evening. Considering the press camped outside your home, I thought it wiser to interview you here."

"Ask," Kingston rasped.

"You and Mrs. Kingston were married late October."

"What does that have to do with her abduction?"

"Until we know who abducted her and why, I consider every question and answer relevant to the investigation."

"It's obvious why," Kingston growled. "They want money."

"But why Mr. Amsel's money? You're the husband and the wealthier relation."

"I've hired you to answer those questions."

"And it's certainly a noteworthy question," he pressed. "If money were the sole motivator, then reason stands that they'd target your pockets."

"Clearly, they expected me to pay."

"If that were the case, they'd have placed the demand on your doorstep."

"Amsel's residence is easier to manage. I have an iron fence around my property, and able staff to watch the grounds."

"That brings me to another point: The first demand

was addressed to Mr. Amsel. Why didn't you front the money?"

"I've never given in to threats and I won't start now!" A fist pounded the hapless armrest.

Riot leaned back, crossed his legs and interlaced his fingers, making himself comfortable in the echo of Kingston's outburst. He studied the fuming man. Kingston's hair was in perfect order, controlled with oils and dye, his mutton chops touched a square jaw, and his eyes smoldered with determination. Here was a man who was used to issuing threats, not the other way around.

"Even when your wife is involved?" Riot asked calmly.

"Amsel is a proud man," Kingston answered through a thin veneer of control. "The ransom was left on *his* doorstep. I offered the money, he refused, so we compromised. I helped him raise the money by negotiating a property sale. And I hired your agency to find Isobel *discreetly*. As far as I'm convinced, it was money wasted. Your agency has done absolutely nothing. I suspect it was one of your men who fed the story to the press."

"Why would we send a ransom demand to newspapers that targeted our employer?"

"How the devil should I know? It's damn suspicious."

"I agree. However, for the time being I prefer to deal with the first demand first," Riot said, with a hint of whimsy. "How did you and your wife spend your first Christmas, Mr. Kingston?"

"We hosted a dinner party."

"I'm told she had planned to visit her family."

"Plans change," Kingston stated. "A wife's duty is to her husband, not to her family. I decided the day would be better spent cultivating business connections."

"Was the dinner a success? Were your guests happy

and was your wife a perfect hostess?"

Kingston's eyes narrowed. "There were no complaints. Isobel did nothing to embarrass me, if that is what you're asking."

"Were you worried that she would embarrass you?"

"My wife is young," Kingston grunted. "It was her first society dinner as hostess. I didn't know what to expect."

"You married her, Mr. Kingston."

"I'm a man with needs. I did not marry for love and neither did she. Our match was beneficial to both parties."

"Your benefits are quite obvious, but what of hers?"

"Money."

"She hardly came from a family of paupers," Riot observed.

"Her father made a number of regretful choices. His business was failing. Isobel was accustomed to a certain standard of living that she wasn't prepared to give up."

"And yet your wife enrolled at university."

"Merely a youthful whim that proved too much work," Kingston chuckled.

"You met over the summer?"

"I don't think our relationship is of your concern."

"Curiosity has always been my greatest failing."

"Failure, of any kind, is unacceptable."

"So is avoidance," Riot stated, then switched directions. "Tell me about the 26th."

"There was a fire at one of my warehouses in Oakland. I took the ferry over to assess the damage."

"What time did you leave the house?"

"I left at once—6:45 and caught the 7:15 to Oakland."

"You were already dressed?"

"Of course I was," Kingston harrumphed. "I instruct-ed my man March to cancel our plans for luncheon and I left."

"For a warehouse fire?"

"The contents, Mr. Riot," Kingston explained through strained teeth. "Imported textiles. A chink threw his fire-crackers through one of the windows, and I'll be damned if the damage comes out of my pockets."

"Did you speak with your wife before leaving?"

"Briefly," Kingston said. "I had no idea she intended to visit her family after the luncheon was canceled."

The edge of Riot's lip quirked. "But she wished to spend Christmas in Sausalito."

"Playing hostess taxed her."

"Ah, yes, of course. You described her as 'delicate' in an earlier interview. In what regards?"

"She lays in quite a bit. Pampered, is what she is." Kingston picked up a cigar, clipped the end, and stuck the Havana between his lips.

"Does she have a regular physician?"

"None of your concern." The beast stirred with agitation in his chair. The flame in his hand wavered.

"Your wife's safety is my concern," Riot countered. "Does your wife have a medical condition?"

"Hysterics, nervousness, name your ailment." Kingston waved his cigar. "The usual afflictions of women folk."

"You weren't aware she intended to visit her family?"

"I said as much."

"Did her lady's maid know?"

"She doesn't keep a regular lady's maid."

Riot frowned. "A pampered lady without a maid?"

"Who can say with women." Kingston shrugged a mighty shoulder.

"Why did your wife take a hack? Surely you keep a carriage for her?"

"I was in a hurry so I took the phaeton. The landau was being repaired—a broken spring."

"When did you return from Oakland?"

"I took the 12:00 to San Francisco, and went straight to my office on Market."

"When did you return home?"

"The evening—5:00 pm."

"And what did you do when you discovered your wife had gone?"

"I questioned the staff at length."

"Why at length, Mr. Kingston?"

Kingston frowned, a darkening of his jaw and brow like a gathering storm. Brooding was the word.

"I came home that evening expecting to find my wife waiting for me. She was gone. Of course I questioned the staff."

"Surely, a 'she left to visit her family' would have alleviated your concerns. Did you telephone her family in Sausalito?" Riot kept his voice low and controlled, forcing the larger man to listen. "Your wife is much younger, Mr. Kingston. You, yourself, said it was a marriage of convenience, not love. It would be understandable for any man to suspect an affair."

"I won't deny it. The thought occurred to me, but that obviously wasn't the case."

"Yet you didn't call her family to confirm?"

"No."

"It would have been a simple matter," Riot observed, reasonably. "Did you make other inquiries on the evening you returned?"

"My wife was abducted. A ransom note was sent. Focus on finding her, and don't pry into my affairs." Kingston ruthlessly crushed his cigar into an ashtray, and abruptly stood.

"Do you have any enemies, Mr. Kingston?"

"No one in particular."

"Not even rival Chinamen?"

Heavy footsteps marched towards the door, followed by a booming slam.

5

The Dreaming Detective

ZEPHANIAH RAVENWOOD SAT ON his throne, impassive as ever, watching his partner shuffle a deck of cards without his customary finesse. It would make the second deck he'd ruined that evening.

Atticus Riot was neither impassive nor calm. While emotion was regrettably commonplace, unrest was not, and therefore troubling to Ravenwood.

"The deck will remain the same no matter how many times you shuffle. It will still contain fifty-two cards."

Riot stopped his restless shuffling. He looked into the humorless eyes across from him. The light from the fire danced in their dark reflection. As always, Ravenwood's words held deeper significance. Riot tapped his abused deck square, stood, and placed it on the mantel.

"You are angry," Ravenwood noted dryly. The severe man interlaced his long fingers in thought. "We solved a case, brought a murderer to justice, and yet you appear dissatisfied. Usually you are eager to celebrate, while I am not. I need no company, my boy, go do whatever it is you do—I suspect women."

"There's no cause to celebrate," Riot murmured.

"As I have been saying these past twenty years."

Riot bestowed annoyance on his partner. "With this case," he clarified, knowing full well that Ravenwood knew it too. "As you said, no matter how many times I shuffle the deck, it won't change the cards."

"Not my precise words but—"

"We haven't changed a thing, Ravenwood. Those children are still dead!"

The large man in his throne was unruffled by Riot's frustration. "The dead have been avenged."

"It doesn't change a thing," Riot repeated, running a hand over his face. "I'm tired."

"Sleep would remedy your ailment."

"I'm tired of this. Of finding the killer after the fact!"

"We have, on occasion, prevented a crime—including murder."

Riot closed his eyes briefly. There was truth in his words, but today, of all days, truth wasn't enough. He took a calming breath and resumed his seat.

"You will recall, I am sure, the day we met."

"Don't patronize me, my boy."

"I had a certain reputation as a gambler: The Undertaker's Friend. You said while I was a friend to death, you were his avenger. Well, I'm tired of avenging. I'd rather save people while they're still breathing."

"We took a brutal murderer off the streets. He'll soon hang because of our efforts. Preventable measures have their own rewards."

"And what of the others?" Riot asked. "All those children being peddled like cattle."

"You can join Father Caraher's war and attempt to blockade the *brothels and cow yards. You'll be the first ex-gambler, ex-detective, turned preacher."*

"Don't mock me, Ravenwood," he warned.

"We are detectives, we see to justice. We don't change the world. That's a job for the preachers, police, and politicians."

"They're not doing their jobs."

"Have they ever?" Ravenwood asked, gripping the armrests and leaning forward. He resembled a snowy owl about to swoop on its prey. "You are allowing emotion to cloud judgment. As I have often reminded you through the course of our partnership—that is never wise."

"I'm tired of finding the mutilated corpses of children thrown into the bay."

"While I admit this last case had a number of unpleasant aspects, balance has been restored. The rest of this…" Ravenwood waved an impatient hand at his partner, "…is clearly a personal vendetta."

"It's not personal."

"Your history strongly indicates otherwise."

"My mother has nothing to do with this," Riot said through his teeth.

"Did I mention your mother?"

If there was ever a man to get under his skin, it was Zephaniah Ravenwood. Riot stared at his partner, resisting the urge to pummel him with his walking stick. Instead he stood, recovered his deck of cards, and resumed his shuffling. This time the cards whispered in his skilled hands.

"I'll humor you, Riot," Ravenwood stated, leaning back in his chair. "Let's consider your proposal. The Tongs run the slavery and opium markets. Both lucrative, both supported by politicians and police officials who benefit from graft. Chinatown's own Six Companies have long worked against both the slave trade and vice, providing the police with needed information about criminals. But the police *only make token raids, as money finds its way into their pockets."*

It was the bitter truth, and Riot had no answer.

"I'll say again, we are not lawmen; we are detectives. Have you forgotten why we left Pinkerton's?"

"This isn't about strike breaking."

"What do you propose to do?"

"Sever the head," Riot stated coolly.

"It's a twelve-headed beast. Sever one and another will take its place."

"Then I'll bring them all down."

"Alone?"

"I'll find honest patrolmen."

"It's a dangerous game."

"Life is full of risks."

⚜

Atticus Riot sat straight up in his narrow bed. His heart was galloping. The darkness unnerved him. He tossed his sweat-soaked blankets aside and hurried over to the windows. Shoving the curtains aside, he fought with the latch, and threw a window open.

Cool, biting air slapped him into the present. He clutched the windowsill and took great gulps of air. His temple throbbed.

Riot closed his eyes, and focused on breathing. Silvery fog touched his skin with a cooling caress. He was grateful for its comfort.

The dream was never-ending, repeating night after night. It was always the beginning of a nightmare—one he had lived. He'd survived while his best friend and partner had not.

6

The Only Daughter

A FRENZIED BELL SLICED through the stillness. The intruding demand rescued Isobel Kingston from an uneasy slumber. Mercurial eyes darted around the unfamiliar bed chamber. Silks, velvet, Parisian wall prints, and rare woods —opulence in the extreme. A wave of nausea hit her. She closed her eyes, gathering her strength.

A booming voice pushed against the walls, invading her cozy nest. Footsteps marched down the hallway, amplified tenfold in the hollowed home. The floorboards shuddered, and Isobel forced herself to relax.

The door opened without inquiry. "There's been a fire. A warehouse across the bay."

Isobel lowered the comforter and blinked at the towering man in her doorway. "How dreadful. No one was injured, I hope?"

Alex scowled at her simpering tone. In answer, he softened his own voice—all politeness. "None. We'll have to cancel our plans."

"Such a pity," Isobel yawned daintily. "I so enjoy the Palace. I'm sure you'll manage everything perfectly."

"I always do, my dear." Alex Kingston smiled like a great grizzled bear before shutting her bedroom door.

Isobel listened to his retreating footsteps. When they faded, she exhaled, slow and controlled. Steeling herself, she pushed back the covers and rose. Ignoring the waiting slippers, she walked across the plush carpet on bare feet, nudging the curtain away from the wall—enough to watch the street.

Fog swirled lazily in the early morning. A lonely bread wagon trundled past, and five minutes later the phaeton pulled out of the carriage house, stopping at the foot of the mansion steps. Alex appeared, climbed into the carriage, and ordered the driver to the ferry building.

Isobel watched the phaeton roll out of the gates onto California. When horse and carriage disappeared over the crest of cobblestones, she exhaled, resting her forehead against the wall.

The air was cold. She stirred, padded across the spacious bedroom, and retrieved her robe, slipping into its warmth and pausing at her reflection. Slowly, as if being pulled by an unseen force, she walked over to the dressing table and sat in front of the mirror.

Her golden plait gleamed, shimmering in the pale light and clashing with the room's explosion of gilt and polish. Eyes, ever shifting, roamed over an unfamiliar face.

Sharp bones, hard lines, and a frown that held a remnant of sincerity.

"You're an utter fool, Bel," she whispered. Resigned, she reached for her brush. Her chin rose, her knuckles turned white. *"One must be cunning and wicked in this world,"* she explained to her reflection, as she had explained every day for the past three months. Only today was different.

Today she would play the coward.

7

The Whispering Wind

"WHAT THE HELL ARE we standing out here for, A.J.?" Tim blew into his hands, rocking back and forth on his heels.

"You should be accustomed to the cold by now. You spent years prospecting by Sutter's Fort," Riot reminded the older man.

The *Eureka* plowed through a bleak horizon, void of place and time, but mostly of warmth.

"And I swore I'd never freeze again. This cold's wet. I'm too old to be standing out here when there's perfectly good seats inside a warm cabin."

A sharp breeze cut through the fog, stirring the veil, slicing through wool and cutting to the bone. Tim shivered, thrust his hands in his pockets, and then retreated into his peacoat. He looked like a grumpy turtle.

Riot gazed into the disturbance, catching a fleeting glimpse of Mount Tamalpais—the maiden in repose. They were nearing Sausalito.

The ferry slowed, its black stack coughed and churned a steamy exhale. A horn blared, rousing passengers inside the main cabin. They moved like ghosts behind windows blurred with heat.

"According to the paper, the weather was similarly dreary last week."

"As it was the week before, and just about all summer." Tim had a point. The Silver Mistress came and went as she pleased, no matter the season.

"After speaking with Mr. Kingston, I called on the Worth residence."

"How many buttons were on the lady's coat?"

"Eight, but that wasn't the interesting part," Riot said with a hint of excitement. "The coat was dreary because it was grey and the cut was similar to a peacoat—hardly fashionable."

"It *was* cold."

"Yes, but she was married to a man who could afford the latest Parisian fashions. Given the length and thickness of the coat, I inquired as to how they noticed the cut and color of her dress. It seems there were two empty seats across from her. When mother and daughter entered the cabin, Mrs. Kingston wasn't wearing the coat as the main cabin is heated."

Tim looked wistfully at the vision of faraway warmth.

"Drunk with holiday good cheer, the women complimented Mrs. Kingston on her attire, and attempted to engage her in further conversation. They thought her rude because she didn't answer. But our lady was no such thing."

"Sounds rude to me," Tim defended.

"Uncommunicative is not rude," Riot said. "She immediately donned her coat, which had been draped over her carpet bag, gathered her belongings, and left."

"And moved to another seat."

"I pressed the mother on that point."

"I didn't think to question it," Tim muttered, attempting to scowl at himself.

"The Worths did not actually see Mrs. Kingston take another seat. They assumed she did, because she walked towards the stern of the ferry. As you can see, there is a door leading to the cabin deck, as well as stairs leading down to the main along with the ladies retiring room."

"I questioned the matron on board," Tim added quickly. "She didn't recall Mrs. Kingston inside the retiring room."

"So it's very likely that Mrs. Kingston, after donning her sensible coat that clashed with her otherwise fashionable attire, walked outside on a day like this one, and endured the cold."

"Why are we doing the same, then?"

"We are observing."

"There's nothing to observe."

"Precisely," Riot said, making a sweeping gesture with his stick. "Not even a deckhand, Tim. The crew is focused on the cabin's passengers and their destination. And currently, the majority of the passengers are crowding around the exit waiting to disembark."

"With their backs to us."

"Very unlikely to notice a lone figure in a 'dreary' grey long coat, especially with the steam-coated windows and this fog."

The two men gazed at the empty deck. One traced the pattern on the knob of his stick, and the other shifted impatiently from foot to foot.

"The question," Riot mused, "is what drove our young lady outside. Was she upset, did something startle her, or was she lured?"

"Can't think of what might have startled her," Tim said. "If it was a rough sort of fellow, she'd likely have stayed with the crowd. Anyone with sense would."

"Fear doesn't always coincide with good sense." Riot gestured over the railing at the main deck below and the open-ended stern. "Two ends for convenience and time— so the captain doesn't have to turn the ship around. It makes for a quick exchange of cargo and passengers, all of whom are eager to make train connections."

"Twenty minutes to unload, clean, and load before the ferry heads back to San Francisco."

"Plenty of time for mischief." Riot leaned against the rail and contemplated the deck, deep in thought. "For the sake of clarity, let's focus on the first ransom note. We know our abductors are either watermen or they hired a boat and its captain. With enough forethought, it would be a simple matter for a small boat to tie off on the pier, wait for the ferry to dock, row up to the stern, and spirit away our young lady."

"Someone would notice," Tim protested.

"In this fog?" The horn blared, declaring the port reached. "With this noise—the horn and paddle? Mrs. Kingston could have screamed, and no one would have been the wiser."

"But all that takes planning," Tim said. "No one knew she was leaving until she asked the household to summon a hack."

"Shortly after her husband left at 6:45. The hackman said she seemed to be in a hurry."

"You think she was trying for the 7:30 ferry?"

"I'm not sure," Riot admitted, "but what we do know is she was on the 9:00. That leaves nearly two hours unaccounted for. Perhaps she was being watched, and while she was lingering around the ferry building her abductors wired ahead."

"We're not sure she was abducted on the ferry," Tim argued, playing the Devil's advocate. "With this many people disembarking and boarding, one woman would be easy to miss. I'd wager she was taken on Water Street."

"You've been focusing your inquiries along the waterfront for a week and have come up dry."

"Because it makes sense," Tim defended. "Otherwise it's too complicated for my liking."

"You've always preferred games of chance, Tim. One roll of the dice—take it or leave it. I prefer strategy. And there is always an advantage when you know your opponent."

"This abduction theory of yours involves a lot of knowing, A.J. I've known you all your life, and I couldn't have predicted you'd try to freeze me to death."

A voice came on the wind, a whisper from the past, '*Too complicated, my boy.*' Riot shivered at the sonorous rasp, and said aloud, to chase the voice away, "I don't know about that. You know what a thoughtful man I've grown into."

As the ferry settled into its dock, Riot peered over the rail. A few disreputable rowboats, tied to ladders, bobbed between the piers.

He glanced along the murky shoreline. There was certainly no shortage of docks in Richardson's Bay. Vague shadows stretched into still waters, like wooden fingers sifting through the morning tides.

"Did you know that Mrs. Kingston did not employ a regular lady's maid?" Riot asked.

"Yes."

"You don't find it peculiar? Alex Kingston belongs to the most exclusive gentleman's club on the west coast. He's in deep waters with the Big Four, some of the wealthiest men in the country, and yet his wife doesn't employ a lady's maid."

"A regular one."

"Even more curious," Riot mused. "An irregular maid implies that she has need of one."

"I'm not following. How does this figure in with her abduction?"

"*The greatest thing in the world is to know how to belong to oneself,*" Riot murmured, and took one last look at the empty deck, then abruptly spun on his heel, striding towards the narrow stairwell that led to the main deck.

Tim blew out a breath, ruffling his mustache, and launched himself after the elusive man. Like his mentor, Atticus Riot's thoughts were his own.

The forward ramp was down, spewing out the contents of the main deck. Harnesses shifted, horses flicked their ears, and a rattle of wagons filled the cavernous hold. Tim wistfully watched an electric automobile drive down the ferry ramp. A distant train whistle blew impatiently and a delivery wagon lurched forward. Riot was perched on the back of it, legs dangling, eyes downcast, contemplating either his shoes or the deck boards.

Tim sprinted forward, and hopped on board, settling himself beside Riot as the wagon rattled off the ferry.

"Our lady was impeccably garbed save for a dubious

coat and carpet bag," Riot began, "but still eye-catching. Someone, I hope, would have noticed an unconscious woman being carried down the gangplank."

"They could have stuck a gun against her ribs or it could be like I suspect—she was 'napped on Water Street."

"A possibility with a number of drawbacks," Riot said, tapping his stick against his shoe. "Firstly, Sausalito is a relatively small town, especially for someone who spent her life there. Revolver or no, I doubt the abductors were willing to risk someone recognizing her. For a girl who grew up in Sausalito, she's bound to know people on Water Street. Secondly, in my experience, women are utterly unpredictable."

"That's exactly the sort of nonsense Ravenwood would have spouted," Tim grumbled.

"Fear and respect are two entirely different matters. A woman's mind is not an easy thing to read."

"And no two of them alike."

"And so each remains a delightful source of mystery," Riot said with a hint of humor. "I'd like you to question the staff of the *Eureka* again. Ask if anyone noticed a boat drifting past the stern of the ferry while it was docked on the 26th, and whether such a thing is common or not."

"That'd be a stretch of their memory."

"Worth the attempt. And while you're at it, ask after any groups, especially inebriated ones. I imagine there were quite a few sailors trickling back to port after a night of Christmas revelry, or ill, faint—"

"I get your drift," Tim interrupted, hopping off the wagon bed. As the wagon rumbled down the dirt road, he shouted, "Where you off to?"

"I've been at sea for a month. Desperation calls," Riot crooned.

"Gawd." Tim wrinkled his nose.

"Never fear, I'll get three bottles of ruin—one for courage and two for despair."

"You'll need it, boy."

8

A Discordant Hive

TUESDAY, DECEMBER 26, 1899
EIGHT DAYS EARLIER

ISOBEL GLIDED DOWN THE staircase. Her eyes caught the color of her dress, mirroring the fine green wool. The maid, who had insisted on carrying her carpet bag, hurried on her heels. She was out of breath.

As expected, a butler whose head was as shiny as his shoes waited at the landing. Isobel was not surprised. Very little escaped March's notice, but then it was the little things she was hoping for today.

"I'm visiting my family, March," Isobel announced, slipping on a pair of kidskin gloves.

"The landau is being repaired, ma'am. An issue with the rear spring, I'm afraid. If you'll wait—"

"Don't be absurd," Isobel countered, adjusting her hat in a gilded mirror. "A cab will do. It's only down the hill."

"As you wish, ma'am." March nodded to the footman, who hurried outside to carry out their lady's wish.

"Will you be wanting your cream coat or the fur, ma'am?"

"The grey if you please, Mabel."

"The grey?" Puzzlement shone on her dark face.

"I'm only visiting family. And it's cold. I want to walk in the hills," Isobel explained with feeling. With a resigned air, Mabel disappeared into the cloak room, and reappeared with the heavy long coat.

Isobel allowed herself to be helped into the warm wool, smiled at the maid's disapproving frown, and picked up her carpet bag. Straight-backed and determined, she walked briskly towards the front doors. March whisked the doors open.

"Kindly inform Mr. Kingston that I'll be spending the New Year with my family. He's welcome to join me if he likes."

March arched a brow. "As you wish, ma'am."

Isobel watched the hack roll up the drive. The footman trotted alongside, then hurried forward to help her with her bag. She took his offered hand and stepped into the cab, arranging her skirts.

March paid the fare in advance, and the hackman nudged the horse with a gentle tap. As the carriage rolled through the iron gates, her heart stayed steady—strangely so.

The rising sun broke through the fog, shining on the long, straight street and the city below. San Francisco was wide awake. Thousands of strangers moved through it like a discordant hive, one worker competing against the other, all striving after golden sweetness.

The cable cars rolled past, pulled along the street by thick cables under the cobble stones, while carriages and automobiles sprinted ahead, weaving in and out of plodding delivery wagons. Bicyclists and cart drivers risked life and limb, and pedestrians tempted chance each time they crossed the street. And all the while, Isobel's eyes darted from one stranger to the next, searching faces, noting vehicle and drivers, gripping the handle of her carpet bag, waiting for the perfect moment.

An overturned hay wagon, a tangle of spokes, and a smashed automobile provided an opportunity. The hackman slowed his cab to navigate the chaos. Amid shouts and whistles and a hundred eyes focused on the commotion in the middle of the intersection, Isobel slipped out of the cab and hurried across the path of an oncoming cable car.

By the time the cable car had passed, Isobel Kinston had faded into the city, joining thousands of indifferent strangers.

✥

The woman in green reappeared on Market, stepping off a cable car runner with a flash of ankle and calf. Furtively she scanned the teeming street from beneath her wide brimmed hat. As usual, the base of Market was madness. Cabs were swarmed, Chinese porters wove through the throng with heavy trunks on their backs, children bawled, and men cursed, all in a frenzied rush to reach their destinations.

Isobel plunged into the fray, slipping through the crowd with accustomed ease. A tall shadow enveloped her.

The ferry building sat at the foot of Market like a mono-lithic starting line, and whether one was starting or finish-ing, the world waited beyond its doors. High on the top of its tower, a round eye watched the race, marking time with two revolving hands.

The clock approached nine o'clock and Isobel walked steadily towards the door. She glanced in the window, searching the reflection for her faithful shadows. They were absent. Her lips formed a severe line and delicate brows drew closer together for comfort. Shaking off a sudden chill, she readjusted the long coat hanging over her arm and allowed a gentleman to open the door. With a slight nod, she walked into the busy hub and took her place in the ladies queue.

Something was stirring, something scratched at the inside of her breast, and for the first time since waking, uncertainty reared its ugly head.

9

Red and Younger

ATTICUS RIOT STROLLED DOWN the pier, appreciating the steady click of his stick on the dock planks. Conducting an investigation, he mused, was not unlike fishing. Any detective could cast his figurative net over the sea of humanity, but it was a skilled detective who chose the right time and place, rarely coming up empty. Riot moved towards a promising spot.

Two fishermen, one young and one old, sat mending their nets, arguing over politics and tides. In Riot's experience, there were two types of old men: those who kept their words close and those who threw them at anyone within range. He was hoping for the latter.

The men smelled of tar and fish, and their words mingled with the surf like old friends. When Riot stopped at the end of the dock, their conversation died. Sharp eyes left their nets, appraising and subsequently dismissing him, before returning to their livelihood and conversation.

That is exactly what Atticus Riot wanted. The lure was cast. There was nothing to do but wait.

He stood for a time, surveying Richardson's Bay. A motley fleet of boats filled the bay: arks, yachts, three-masted steamers, and feluccas all mingled on the still water.

Across the bay, a long stretch of inhospitable shore rose from the water. A few suicidal mansions perched on the cliff's edge, risking death daily for beauty's sake. The cliffs shared the water with Angel Island: the guardian of the western gate. The island bristled with cannon batteries and troops, inspection and quarantine stations, ready to defend San Francisco on all fronts.

A rough voice breached the silence, interrupting Riot's consideration. "We've each of us—one and all—given our story to your ilk."

Riot turned towards the voice. The bent old man sat on a crate, gnarled fingers moving confidently over his net. He was a bundle of wool, huddled under a thick peacoat.

"I do not represent police or press." Riot produced his card, stamped boldly with a raven. The fisherman glanced at the card, and then at his younger companion, who leaned forward to read what the older could not.

"Says he's a detective by the name of Atticus Riot with Ravenwood Agency." The younger man wore no coat. His sleeves were rolled up to the elbow. Thick, dark hair traveled up his forearms, disappeared beneath his shirt, and sprang up at his throat. A swath of leathery skin, two bright green eyes, and a twice broken nose were the only things distinguishing man from bear.

The old man removed his cap and regarded Riot,

slowly perusing the detective's fedora, trimmed beard, silver waistcoat, and pinstriped trousers, as if Riot were a tailor's window model.

"Your name is known to me," the old man announced, nodding in satisfaction. "I've not heard it spoken in some years."

"I've been abroad," Riot supplied. "I'm afraid your name isn't known to me."

"They call me Red, and this here's Younger."

Riot touched the brim of his hat in greeting.

"You're looking for that Amsel girl, aren't ya?" asked Younger.

"I am."

"An honest family of boatbuilders." Red nodded down the long stretch of beach where a forest of masts clustered around docks. "Mr. Amsel did a fine job when he took over the Saavedra shipyards."

"A fine winemaker, too, or so I hear," Younger threw in.

"A local label?"

"Up north in the valley, but we count him as one of our own, being he's married into the area."

"And all his wine moves through our ports," Younger finished.

"Most boats, too," Red grunted.

"Do the Saavedra shipyards specialize in yachts?"

"Crab boats." Red thrust his chin towards a nearby pier where crabs were being sold fresh from their traps. "And trawlers, too."

"They make a fine pleasure yacht," Younger added.

"Cater to the 'codfish aristocracy' and their kind," Red grumbled sourly.

"You still going on about that, are you, Red?" Younger

blew out a breath, puffing up his mustache.

Riot sifted through his memory, dredging up a bitter battle for incorporation between Sausalito's hill people and flatlanders. The former had wanted sewer lines and street lamps, while the latter were content with a rougher life, free of taxes and control.

"They couldn't leave well enough alone, now could they?" Red retorted. "And it come just as I feared. Brought in their conveniences, and the codfish started meddlin' in our affairs and fixin' things to suit their whims."

"How so?" Riot asked, leaning against a piling.

"Don't get the man started," Younger grunted, returning to his nets.

"That fire was set on purpose and I won't hear a word edgewise."

"Seven years ago," Younger explained. "He's still going on about a fire seven years past."

"Destroyed most of the waterfront," Red defended to Riot. "And now we have this *Municipal Improvement Club* trying to clean up Water Street."

"It could do with some cleaning."

Red ignored his partner. "It's not right, encroaching on a man's freedoms, and now Amsel's got his girl all mixed up in the mess."

"This has nothing to do with her kidnapping," Younger sighed.

"Like hell it doesn't. She went off and married that codfish Kingston. Any man with more money than is good for him lays his hat where it shouldn't be."

"The *Municipal Improvement Club*?" Riot asked.

"The hill people and merchants decided the poolrooms were bad for the town, so they started a reform movement, trying to reverse the town's decision to legalize gambling.

And I can't disagree. I won't allow my wife to walk down Water Street in the evenings."

Red began to chuckle. "You weren't here in forty-nine. Those days make the waterfront seem like a luxury hotel."

"Nothing wrong with a little change," Younger stated.

"You don't care for Alex Kingston?" Riot nudged the conversation in the direction he desired.

"Red doesn't care for any man with money in his pockets," Younger answered, eyeing the tailored cut of Riot's suit.

"Not true," Red grunted. "Only the ones who presume to use their money to steal my freedoms."

"Your freedoms?" Younger asked in exasperation. "Well, I take offense to rigging elections and buying votes."

"Were the elections rigged?"

"Course they were. Sausalito's the only town where poolrooms are legal. But I don't take offense to restoring a freedom where it shouldn't have been taken in the first place. A man should be able to gamble if he likes."

"Whatever your view," Younger countered, "I'm throwing my hat in with Amsel and his lot."

"Take my advice," Red advised Riot. "Don't involve yourself. You'll end up like Amsel and his girl."

"You're of the opinion that Mrs. Kingston was abducted because of her father's involvement with the reform movement?"

"Damn straight," Red nodded.

"Your reasoning is as sound as this dock," Younger argued. "The demand in the newspaper was aimed at Kingston, and he's not part of the club—he's not even part of this town."

"He married an Amsel didn't he?"

"Makes Isobel a Kingston, not the reverse," Younger

retorted.

"She'll always be our Miss Isobel."

"You are both acquainted with Mrs. Kingston?"

Red began chortling. "See Younger's nose there?"

Riot nodded. "It's quite crooked."

"Amsel's girl did that—years ago now."

"Before her parents sent her to Europe to be tamed," Younger explained. The swath of leather between beard and brow turned a rosy hue.

"Tamed," Red spat for emphasis. "As tame as a shark waiting for the fool to remove his hook."

Riot glanced at the younger man. The sea had worn him beyond his years and the broken nose lent him an air of brutishness that conflicted with his thoughtful words.

"You grew up with her brothers," Riot surmised.

"That I did," Younger confirmed. "Merrik, the second to youngest, was my best mate."

"Isobel being the youngest?"

"And her brother Lotario. They're twins. She's full of spitfire and ice," Younger said with a grin. "Didn't ever take to being told to leave well enough alone." Riot waited for the man to continue, nodding towards his nose, and Younger obliged his curiosity.

"Isobel had a habit of disguising herself as her twin brother Lotario. It was a game they played. Couldn't tell the one from the other, if they decided to trick a man.

"While sailing around the bay with Lotario, Merrik and I were set to outdo one another. We got it in our foolish heads to swim to Angel's Island. Course when Lotario decided to swim too—well, we found out otherwise. It was Isobel. I told her that's no swim for a girl and she made to go anyhow. So, Merrik grabbed her, intending to lock her in the cabin." Younger wrinkled his nose. "She kicked him square and knocked what God gave man. Then she turned right around and walloped me in the nose. Merrik and me weren't much for the swim after that."

"It's bad luck is what it is, a female sharing a womb with a male," Red intoned sagely. "She was wild as the sea."

"Is," Younger corrected. "And whatever hoodlum snatched her, I'm sure she's giving him hell. She's bound to come home."

"One way or another," Red sighed.

"We wish you all the luck, Mr. Riot," said Younger.

"I'm sure you've both been over it with the police and press, but did you see Mrs. Kingston, or anything suspicious on the 26th?"

Both men looked at the other, clearly startled.

"The 26th?" they asked as one.

"Thought she went missing on the 30th—the day before that awful letter in the papers."

Riot readjusted his spectacles. The town might be close-knit, but Amsel and Kingston had managed to keep the first ransom demand to themselves. Had Amsel shared the first demand with the police after the second hit the newspapers? If he had, then the authorities were doing a fair job of keeping it quiet. And as for Tim's questioning— well, he was as sly as they came. When Tim was involved, no one ever suspected they were being grilled for information.

"Could have been anytime within the past seven days." Both men considered his words, fingers moving over familiar nets of their own accord, aiding their mental recollections.

"No." Younger shook his head. "Can't say as I did. And as for anything suspicious, can't say anything to that.

This is a port of destination for all those heading north. Plenty of strangers coming and going all day long."

"Moorin' their damn yachts every which way, like they own the bay," Red grumbled.

"Is Old Sue known to either of you?"

"Maybe to Red," Younger cackled.

The older man glared at his partner. "She was a looker back before your day. Leave her be, boy. Life takes its toll on us all."

"I'm told she's a regular at the docks."

"That she is," Red nodded, "as permanent as these piers."

"You can usually find her roaming the waterfront, pestering the saloons or looking to earn some money any which way she can."

"Was she here on the 26th?" Riot asked. "That would have been last Tuesday."

Red put down his net and withdrew his pipe and pouch.

Younger shrugged. "I can't say, but now that you mention it, I haven't seen her all week."

Riot waited as Red packed and tamped his bowl, struck a match, and puffed on the stem. When a thin line of fragrant smoke rose from his lips, he spoke. "Sue was at the docks that day. I gave her a small crab that got caught in our nets."

"Did you notice anyone speaking with her?" Riot pressed.

"Sue approached every boat on these docks. Can't say as any stands out."

"If anything comes to mind—anything at all—send me a wire, if you would." Riot handed over his card. "Does Old Sue keep rooms in town?"

"A shanty, at the far end of Whaler's Cove," Younger said, nodding in a southerly direction. "Back in the trees."

Riot tipped his hat in gratitude and made to leave, but stopped short at a sudden thought. "I assume Miss Isobel swam to the island?"

Younger chuckled. "That she did. There and back in under two hours."

The edge of Riot's lip quirked. "I thought so," he murmured.

10

A Cornered Queen

ISOBEL SANK GRATEFULLY ONTO the padded seat. There were, she mused, advantages to being female on a crowded ferry boat. Gentlemen readily offered their seats.

She set her carpet bag on the floor and laid her coat over its bulky contours. As she tugged off her gloves, she watched the travelers file inside the cabin, taking note of every face along with their mannerisms as her mind flew, moving facts like pieces on a chessboard.

A horn blared, signaling their departure. The great paddle churned and the sea caught the boat.

The noisy cabin made her temples throb. Where were her shadows? They should have been waiting nervously at the ferry building. Perhaps Alex's ego had finally made room for trust? Or had he simply lost interest in his new bride? The hunt was over and her compliance had become dull? Her mind skipped. Had her ruse worked? An ominous thought lurked just out of reach, lost in the tumult of conversation.

Something niggled, something scratched. And a shrill voice shattered the thought.

"I say, Miss?"

Isobel blinked. A pair of eyes snapped into focus. Polite inquiry that was quickly becoming forbearance. Two identical noses poked from a swath of furry hats and coats. One young, and one older. Their identical postures on the seats opposite named them mother and daughter.

"My daughter paid you a compliment, Miss."

"It's a lovely dress," the complimenting daughter repeated.

Isobel's brows twitched in irritation. The answer had been within reach. The din of conversation, blaring horn, and the wet chug of the paddle washed over her, bursting between her ears. Abruptly she rose, slipped into her gloves and reassuring coat, plucked her bag from the floor and flew towards the closest exit.

The faces—all the faces and eyes and bodies clamored for attention. She threw open the door.

Cool, sweet relief slapped her in the face, filling her lungs and mind with clarity. Isobel sought the farthest point from distraction, pressing herself against the taffrail, leaning over the side, drinking deep draughts of cool air as she stared down at hypnotic waves.

Amid the swirls, white caps and ebbing valleys, the missing thought swam into view. Her throat caught, eyes widened, and the scratching tore open a deluge of alarm.

The chessboard had shifted. She had become the

pawn. With that alarming realization, she turned, finding two towering men and a scarred fist.

The queen was captured.

11

Three for Ruin

OLD SUE'S SHANTY WAS tucked at the base of an ivy-covered cliff. The structure dwelt in shadow, beneath a towering cypress that stretched its branches over the rotting wood, turning day to night. Riot picked his way through reeds, smelling of licorice and damp earth, that stretched over his head. The plank path groaned under his feet, like a cranky manservant announcing a guest.

He mounted the steps and was assaulted by a familiar stench—a sweetly pungent smell that drowned the earth and sea, and crawled down his throat.

Riot nudged the door open with the end of his stick. The room was small. A single chair and table, a shelf and a chipped washbasin, a trunk and a cot. A lump lay on the cot under a legion of flies. From the looks of the bloated shape, Death had come and fled days ago. But where had his old friend gone next?

As if fearing to disturb the corpse, Riot moved into the shanty, leaving the door wide open. He opened the single shuttered window, steeled himself, and turned to the body. Corpses were never pleasant; however, an industrious rat that was gnawing on the fleshier morsels certainly appeared to be enjoying itself.

The old woman lay on her back. She was slowly moving. Maggots, life's ultimate conquerors, had already claimed the woman as their own. Riot pressed a handkerchief to his nose. The gesture didn't soften the smell, but he told himself it helped. He waved the rodent away with his stick, and leaned forward, gazing through a glassy sheen.

Her skin was marbled, blood vessels having turned green and black to form intricate patterns over stretched skin. Fingernails seemed too long as flesh shrank back, and her eyes bulged from their sockets.

'Ashes to ashes, dust to dust,' an old voice swirled in the air.

"Three days gone," Riot murmured in answer. Bile caked her lips and the bedding around her head. Stains saturated her clothing. Riot slipped on his thin black gloves, tucked his stick under his arm, and gently shifted the body. He ignored the pale, groping worms that fell on the filthy mattress and searched for any signs of foul play. There were none. Everything indicated that she had died a drunk's glorious death in bed.

Riot straightened, and frowned at coincidence. The decaying woman on the cot had been the only known connection between Mrs. Kingston's abductors and Sausalito. He turned to study the room. The sparse furnishings appeared to be salvaged goods: a rusty pot-bellied stove, a crate that served as a table, with yarn and darning needles on its top, and a cap that would forever remain unfinished. A few dented pots dangled neatly from their hooks above the chipped washbasin.

Squat gin bottles sat in a neat row on the shelf like triumphant trophies, their labels turned out with pride—a touch of art in despair. Seven chubby little friars smiled cheerfully down on the room. Given the position of the single shutter, morning sunlight would shine through its slats to catch the bottles and grace the depressing room with prisms of color.

Riot's footsteps echoed hollowly on the floorboards as he walked across the room. He stopped in front of the shelf, considering the bottles.

"One for courage," he murmured, brushing a finger along the row of glass. "Two for despair. Three for ruin, and four for fear. Five are all mine, and six I'll sell. Seven for heaven."

The first seven bottles had identical friars.

"Eight is far too late. Nine will buy you time," he continued, tapping two dingy green bottles with flared mouths and no labels.

A Rotterdam stamp was embossed along each bottle's naked side. He plucked a green bottle from its perch, and examined it. A faint cross was etched on its base. He sniffed at the mouth. The smell brought to mind a pine tree. Grimacing, he set it back on the shelf.

Riot turned, eyes traveling over the shack. Death rarely made room for neatness. Surely the old woman had died with a bottle clutched to her shriveled bosom. And indeed she had, or close enough.

The bottle in question had rolled under the cot. "And

ten will get you there," Riot finished the old rhyme, plucking the last from the floor. A cat grinned from the label—Old Tom Gin. He straightened and sniffed at the opening. A woody aroma of spice filled his senses, and a sharp bitter bite followed. He pushed a corner of his handkerchief into the opening, wiped the inside, and pulled it out. The pristine silk was marred by a rusty smudge—laudanum sediment.

12

Of Gin and Bottles

STEADY FOOTSTEPS TAPPED ON wood, and a third click was thrown into the rhythm. The footsteps stopped in front of a saloon. A shadow stood for a time's breath, silhouetted in the doorway—black against the silver daylight. Riot nudged the saloon door open and stepped inside, casually placing a hand behind his back to stop the door's creaky swing.

The saloon felt hollow. Shifting light seeped through cracks in the floorboards and the echo of surf crashed underfoot. Brass gleamed in the half-light. A bar, where polished bottles stood to tempt the stoutest of men, stretched the length of the room. Rough sailors, soldiers, and barflies nursed their drinks and heads. It was early yet. Quiet. But the saloon had all the makings of lively evenings.

A layer of peanut shells covered the floor, cracking under his shoes with every step. From the bowing planks, Riot suspected that a fair number of them were rotted. Not very reassuring for a saloon built over the water, especially for a man who could not swim.

He removed his hat and placed it on the bar, nodding to the bartender, a thin, crisp man with spectacles and a pair of mutton chops that were striving to meet across a pointed chin.

"Your pleasure for the morning?"

"I've a taste for gin," Riot replied, adjusting his spectacles to peruse the selection on the shelves. A cheery Black Friar waved at him from a Plymouth label. London's Royal Guard marched across the Beefeaters, and Holland's elephant was stamped permanently on a bottle of Genever. All the bottles were new, nothing like the dull green case bottles with flared lips in Old Sue's shanty.

"Do you stock Old Tom?"

"Too sweet," the bartender explained.

"I'll have the Plymouth." Riot tossed down five cents. In one smooth motion, the bartender plucked the bottle from its perch, righted a shot glass, popped the cork and poured, stopping just shy of the rim. Riot tossed the gin down his throat. The smooth, inoffensive liquid washed away the rotting woman, leaving a soft earthiness that lingered on his tongue.

"Sweeter than some," Riot noted, conversationally.

"My regulars prefer Plymouth."

"Like Old Sue?"

"That she does."

"I'm told she prefers to buy her gin at your fine saloon."

The bartender's eyes narrowed behind his spectacles.

"What business is it of yours, Mr.—"

"Riot, Atticus Riot." He produced his card, sliding it across the varnished bar. "Old Sue is dead. I suspect murder, and I'm to find out who."

The bartender's eyes widened in surprise, and then puzzlement. "Who the hell would want to murder the old lady? She was drinking herself into the grave."

"Someone nudged her sooner than her time," Riot supplied. "She was indeed a regular?"

"When she scraped together enough coins," the bartender confirmed. "And once in a blue moon I'd have work for her: sweeping, mending, scrubbing, and such."

"Did she always purchase Plymouth gin?"

"Far as I know. Never another brand from my stock. Had her particulars, as drunks often do."

"Did she ever add laudanum for an extra kick?"

The bartender shook his head. "Can't see that she could afford such a luxury. And I certainly don't add it—too risky."

"May I see a Genever bottle?"

The bartender shrugged and reached for the square bottle, placing it on the bar. Riot examined the glass, noting the differences: a nearly nonexistent lip, faint vertical lines running the length of the bottle, and a circular indent in the base.

"I ask because I found ten bottles in Old Sue's shanty," Riot explained. "Seven were Plymouth gin, all from the Black Friar's distillery. Two were dark green, dingy, stamped with the Rotterdam mark: squarish but tapered, a sloppy, flared mouth, no label, and an A.H. seal on the shoulder."

"Cross on the base?"

"As a matter of fact, yes."

"Sounds like an old case gin. Newer bottles aren't made with a dip mold anymore. That's how you get the little cross on the base. This bottle here is made with a shingle mold. We call the mouth a Pig's Snout, owing to the shape."

"How old would you estimate the other bottle to be?"

"I can't be sure without examining it, but sounds like it's at least twenty, maybe forty years old."

Riot considered the newer bottle. The bottles in Old Sue's shanty had been carefully cleaned and lined up on the shelf. Three, he could see, might make for a decorative touch to an otherwise drab existence, but the two old bottles didn't fit nicely with that theory.

'*Everything is connected; no matter how small.*' The voice from the past never failed to twist Riot's heart. He had not been idle in Europe. The occasional case had inevitably found its way to his hands, heaping guilt on his shoulders all over again. Each case had brought Ravenwood's memory alive, as if the legend still walked at his side—the very reason Riot had left San Francisco in the first place.

He cleared his throat. "Do you have a regular scavenger?"

"That I do," confirmed the bartender. "Goes by the name of Val—verified union. A weasely Italian fellow who staked his claim to this street. Always wears a paisley yellow waistcoat."

Riot placed a dollar on the bar, slipped on his hat, and touched the brim with gratitude.

13

Trapped

ROPES DUG INTO ISOBEL'S skin. Wood creaked and the floor heaved with her skull. Fish, sweat, stale beer, and salt stung her nostrils. Darkness taunted. Light seeped through a crack, a thin slice of white that seared her eyes. She shut them, fighting past the pulse between her temples, stretching her senses to their limit.

A mound of sacks made up her crude pallet. They were lumpy and damp and smelled of moldy straw. She bit back a moan. Bile rose in her throat, and she swallowed it around a secure gag, concentrating on breathing through her nose. Voices droned above, muffled by wood and the creak of tack. The world lurched, wood greeted wood with a gentle tap. She cracked an eye open, forcing her mind to focus on the shifting sliver of light that swayed to and fro with a gentle rock.

Gathering her strength, she turned her mind to a task, and was rewarded with a single thought: *a poorly maintained boat hold*. The effort cost her dearly. A burst of pain exploded inside her skull. It was every bit as pounding as the fist that had slammed into her. Darkness swallowed her whole.

14

Death's Pleasure

WEDNESDAY, JANUARY 3, 1900

A MAZE OF PILINGS and crab boats hugged the piers. Hulls touched in greeting. Ramshackle wood and crude timber gave way to hillside, where stately houses dotted the steep slope like wild flowers. In the highlands, far from the flats and fish and stench of beer, the air was crisp and ripe with pine and fir.

The sun had chased away the fog. Warmth shone down on Water Street from a sky of crystal, warming the long row of saloons and poolrooms on the flatlands and the grand mansions on the hillsides. Any which way you turned the glass, Sausalito was a perfect study in contrasts.

Atticus Riot strolled along the street, long coat draped over his arm, appreciating the cool breeze and the warming sun. He was regretting the absence of his Panama hat when Tim appeared at his side.

"As always, you send your elders off to do the leg work." Tim fell in step beside the younger man. "I've been blistering these ol' feet of mine, and here I find you taking a stroll."

"It's turned into a lovely day," remarked Riot. "I find Death favors the pleasant."

"The Banana Belt has always been that," Tim agreed.

"Any luck with the ferry crew?"

"Considering the crew work and live on the water, they remembered a good many boats. I've tracked down three Monterey crab boats already. One fancy yacht by the name of *The Gambler* and two rowboats from the yacht club. And I have a list of possibilities the length of my arm. Did Old Sue drink herself into a grave yet?"

"She's been there for some days now, and as a matter of fact, she did drink herself there, but not intentionally. She was murdered, if I'm any judge."

Tim stopped, blinked, and hurried to catch up with Riot's steady gait.

"Murdered?"

"The local police had similar doubts," Riot said dryly. Dealing with the police had reminded Riot why he planned to retire, why he had left San Francisco, and most of all, reminded him of events that drove Ravenwood to his early grave.

"Damn it to hell," Tim swore. "I should have had one of my Vigilance boys keeping an eye on her."

"I doubt your boys would have stopped a drunk from drinking. Do you remember Miss Piggott's Special?" Riot asked.

"Gawd that woman could mix a drink."

"And was handy with a slung shot."

"I do recall," Tim cackled, rubbing his shiny pate beneath his cap. "One of the best crimpers in her day."

"And ruthless."

"So what was the poison?"

"Old Tom's gin, maybe more, and laudanum."

"It's not uncommon for drinkers to put a dose in for an extra kick."

"After speaking with the police, I questioned the barkeep of her favorite haunt. Adding laudanum wasn't her habit. And considering she'd been drinking for twenty years, it seems awfully coincidental that she'd start just after accepting payment to deliver a ransom note."

Tim gave a low whistle. "You think Mrs. Kingston was snatched by some runners turned to ransom?"

"No, I think the ruffians were spooked by the newspaper headlines, and decided to sweep their trail clean."

"That doesn't bode well for Mrs. Kingston."

Riot did not answer. A tremor ran through his bones, shaking his hands. He gripped the silver knob of his weighted stick until his knuckles were white.

This was the part he always dreaded—when Death began laying bodies at his feet like a faithful feline. Atticus Riot was a fair detective, but he was no legend. That distinction belonged to Zephaniah Ravenwood. The late detective had been the real diviner, teasing secrets from the Reaper with a needle-sharp intellect.

Riot, on the other hand, generally blundered his way through an investigation, always one step behind. Not for the first time, or the last, he wished his old friend were alive—not only for his own sake, but for Mrs. Kingston's.

15

A Trail of Gin

A HAND CART TRUNDLED rudely down the dusty road. It stank of everything people discarded on the waterfront. The overloaded cart appeared close to toppling, but on second glance its load was neatly stacked, organized, and categorized. The traveling marvel on wheels was orchestrated by a wiry little man whose mustache hung well past his pointy chin. If further confirmation was needed, the man wore a bright yellow waistcoat, anointing him Val the Weasel.

"Afternoon, sir," a low voice as steady as the sun inserted itself into the ruckus of wheels. Riot tipped his hat and fell in step beside Val, enduring a second assault on his olfactory senses.

"*Una bella giornata,*" Val corrected with feeling.

"A very fine day indeed," agreed Riot. "I'm told you

claim scavenging rights along Water Street."

"I don't claim." Mediterranean eyes blazed. "I have Union papers, eh, from the ferry to the south." Val reached into his breast pocket, never missing a stride, and yanked out a badly creased piece of paper, flourishing it in front of Riot's spectacles. The document proclaimed Valentino Abategiovanni a certified member of the *Scavengers Protective Union.*

"In that case," Riot said, reaching into his own pocket, "I require your expertise." Since Val was a man who liked things official, Riot produced his card. The pasteboard was quickly plucked from his fingertips, studied, and appraised for quality and resale value.

"I require a skilled man, such as yourself, an observant man who knows his trade."

"Better than most," Val boasted.

"I should hope so. I'd hate to have to track down one of your Union brothers."

"No need," Val reassured. "*A vostro comodo.*"

"*Grazie,*" Riot nodded. "Have you ever conducted business with Old Sue?"

"Ah, *sì, la vecchia signora.* Everyone knows her on the waterfront."

"She was murdered," Riot stated, watching Val carefully. The weasel's face crumpled, resembling a despondent rodent. Val stopped, put down his cart, removed his cap and scratched a cross over his breast.

"*Perché?*"

"That is precisely what I'm attempting to answer. Did Old Sue do business with you?"

"The bottles," Val began in the cadence of his native tongue, "they were too heavy for her. Distillers pay twenty-five cents for a bundle of ten. So I carted hers off whenever she gathered enough. As a favor to *la vecchia signora*."

Riot adjusted his spectacles. "That's a pity, Mr. Abategiovanni. Distillers generally pay five cents per bottle. Seems you're being swindled, or Old Sue was at any rate." The accusation hung in the air, heavy and bloated.

Val threw up his arms, bursting the tension. "So I keep half—delivery fees."

"Understandable," Riot soothed with a voice like honey. "To my knowledge, distillers prefer newer bottles, correct?"

"Yes, of course."

"What of the older ones you salvage—say twenty or forty years old?"

Val frowned, slapped his cap on his head, grabbed the cart's handles, and stomped forward. Riot kept pace.

"A glass company across the bay buys old bottles," Val said at length.

"Seems more trouble than fifty cents is worth. A trip like that would cut into your time, and therefore your profits. You're far too smart for that, Mr. Abategiovanni."

Val trudged onwards, tight-lipped and tense.

"I do not have the slightest interest in liquor licenses—or the lack thereof—only justice for *la vecchia signora*," Riot coaxed.

Grudgingly, Val loosened his tongue. "There's a blind pig, south of Whaler's Cove. Boats dock on the old pier."

"*Grazie, signore.*" With this bit of information tucked neatly in his mind, Riot left Val the Weasel to his scavenging.

16

The Blind Pig

ATTICUS RIOT STOOD UNDER a broad willow, appreciating the blind pig's proximity to Old Sue's shanty and Whaler's Cove. The illegal saloon lived in the hull of a salvaged clipper ship. Vine and bramble held the rotting wood upright, like two old friends supporting a drunken comrade.

A rickety dock stretched from the shore, and a tattered red and white flag that might have been a checkered handkerchief in another life fluttered from the dock's end, marking the ruin. Moored boats crowded around the sad pilings, bobbing in the shallow inlet.

His gaze roved north along the shoreline, and then up, traveling over a rumpled landscape that dipped and climbed, until hills peaked high above. Standing on the shoreline and gazing up the sharp slope, the climb appeared more mountain than hill. Somewhere in the countryside of extremes, the Amsel home sat nestled on a hillside above Old Town.

Tim had his strengths. The man could find a needle in a field of haystacks, but he never quite knew what to do with the needle once it was found. And as such, he rarely asked the right questions during an investigation. Riot had one that he sorely wished to ask Old Sue. Regrettably, he could not.

'*If wishes were horses, then the old woman would be alive,*' a dry voice whispered on the breeze.

Riot sighed. Would he ever be free of his mentor's shade? Two branches rubbed together, reminiscent of Ravenwood's rasping chuckle.

Three years gone and Riot was still expecting to find his partner at his side, as aggravating as a stubborn stump. After twenty years of shared investigations, he was left feeling half a man on every case. His life had not felt right since Ravenwood's brutal murder. As long as he continued to investigate, there was no possible way to put the past where it belonged. Looking ahead, a return to the life he'd led before Ravenwood had shoved him into this Godforsaken business, seemed to be his only option.

"One more," Riot murmured. "Then I'll be free."

With retirement near at hand, Riot focused his thoughts. There was work to be done. He draped his long coat over a low branch, gathered up his stick, and unbuttoned his suit coat to adjust the short-barreled Smith & Wesson nestling against his ribs. Calmly, with a stride as casual as the white sails on the bay, he strode towards the disreputable structure.

✥

An inch of sawdust covered the floor. Overturned barrels served as tables and the few chairs in the bar-room looked fit for kindling. The afternoon barflies had already picked themselves out of gutters and dragged themselves inside. As Riot entered, every eye turned to the stranger, watching his progress towards the crude bar.

The bartender's apron was as dingy as his illegal establishment. Riot set his hat on the bar, and nodded to the towering man. A pair of blue eyes stared down a bent nose. The bartender's hair was the color of straw, his cheeks were scarred and his jaw was as square as they came.

"Gin," Riot ordered. "I'm told you brew your own."

"Who told you?" Clearly, from coloring and accent, the man was a Swede.

"Old Sue."

The Swede raised a pale brow.

"I'm something of a connoisseur," Riot smoothly replied. "And I've not had the opportunity to sample a gin that smells like a pine tree."

The Swede smiled, showing off the gaps between his teeth. Tension bled out of the room. Eyes left the back of Riot's head and returned to their cups, deciding that the gentleman in the fancy suit was not there to close down their favorite dive.

The Swede reached under the bar and brought out an aged bottle. The dark glass was scarred and looked battered enough to have weathered the Civil War. "I make it myself," he explained. "I call this one Liquid Bark. It's mixed with whatever I find on the hills."

"As long you're not looking near the dairy farms."

This comment coaxed a rumbling laugh from the

towering man. The Swede uncorked the bottle and waited. "A nickel for the table space," he clarified, as did every saloon that avoided the liquor tax. Riot tossed down his rent and the bartender poured a shot glass. Under the expectant gaze of the Swede, he swallowed his foreboding and sniffed at the contents. Suppressing a wince, Riot gulped down the gin. A forest slid down his throat, and he exhaled its bitter bark.

Small wonder Old Sue hadn't noticed the laudanum in her gin. If she could drink two bottles of this, nothing would give her pause.

"It's like drinking a Douglas fir," Riot coughed. "Can't say I've ever tasted the like."

"That is good," the Swede beamed with pride. "I am the only one who brews it."

"Still," Riot mused, tilting the glass. "I can't imagine you get many requests for this bouquet of bark."

"You'd be surprised."

"Doubtful."

"I sold two bottles last week," the Swede boasted.

"Don't believe it."

"Old Sue bought them."

Riot stifled his surprise. "She's hardly a woman of refined tastes."

"A dollar will buy you rent, and I'll gift you the last."

"I'm afraid you couldn't pay me a dollar to take that gin home," Riot haggled good-naturedly.

"One of a kind," the Swede flashed a grin and placed another old bottle on the bar.

"How much did you pay Old Sue to drink Liquid Bark?" Riot asked, tossing another nickel on the knotted counter.

"You seem awfully interested in the old lady. Did she

steal your heart?"

"After a bottle of your gin, I imagine anything could steal a man's heart," Riot said, leaning against the bar.

"Try this one," the Swede poured another glass. "I raided the spice cabinet."

"I was hoping I'd find Old Sue here," Riot threw out a hopeful line, holding the glass towards the light, studying the questionable sediment floating in the liquid.

"Haven't seen her since last week."

"A pity. I'm looking for two friends. Thought she might have seen the pair on the waterfront. Was anyone with her by chance?"

"I don't pay much attention to faces. And you'd be wise to ignore my customers. I run an amiable establishment."

"It's an amiable enough question." Riot slipped his fingers into his breast pocket and pulled out five dollars. He set it on the bar, loosening the Swede's tongue.

"No one was with Sue when she bought the bottles. She came in, asked for my cheapest stock, so I sold her Liquid Bark for twenty-five cents apiece with a promise she'd return the bottles." The Swede smiled, sliding the bill off the counter and into his willing pocket. "A wise investment, thanks to you."

"Did anyone purchase an Old Tom bottle from you— that day or another?"

The Swede's eyes narrowed. "I think you best leave."

"I paid for my seat and I'm not finished here."

"I don't stock Old Tom."

"You don't much care what drink you stock," Riot countered. The Swede plucked the bottle from the counter and returned it to its place under the bar.

"Or the laudanum you slip into the mix." Riot's eyes

slid from the shot glass in his hand to the Swede. His scarred cheek twitched.

Riot jerked his wrist towards the man's face. Spicy gin splashed over the Swede's eyes. The barkeep reeled, bringing up his hand. Riot cracked his weighted stick over the Swede's rising wrist and snatched the Colt from his numb fingers.

A chair scraped backwards. In one smooth motion Riot hooked his stick around the Swede's neck, slammed him onto the bar, and swiveled, pointing the Peacemaker towards movement in the far corner.

"Stay," he warned. "I'm interested in murder, not tax evasion." Whether it was Riot's quiet command, the revolver in his hand, or the casual way he kept a six foot tall man pinned to the bar with his stick, patrons in the corner resumed their seats.

"The name is Atticus Riot," he announced to the saloon. "I'm a detective, not a lawman." The Swede struggled, and Riot increased pressure on the back of his neck. He waited ten seconds. When he was satisfied the barflies had lost interest, he lowered the gun and his voice. "If you wish to continue 'renting' chairs, then answer my questions. I should inform you that I was a gambler in another life, so if you lie to me, I'll know."

The Swede's eye swiveled in its socket like a crazed horse sensing danger.

"Did you put a dose of laudanum in an Old Tom bottle?"

"Crimping is bad for business. I cater to regulars."

"But you know something," Riot coaxed, increasing the pressure.

"*Cowboy's Rest* on Pacific—maybe the *Whale* or the *Bull*."

"I'm acquainted with both Cowboy Mag and Johnny McNear," Riot said, easing his hold. He leaned against the bar, and uncocked the Colt in consideration. The Swede straightened, rubbing his neck with a grimace.

"Was anyone with Old Sue when she bought the two bottles of Liquid Bark?"

"Not that I noticed, and that's God's own truth."

"Did any boats, whose crew remained on board, moor at your dock?"

"How should I know?"

"Anyone ask about Old Sue?"

"No one except a dandy little prick."

Riot pressed a latch, swung the revolver's cylinder out, and pointed the barrel towards the ceiling. The cartridges fell out of their chambers, clattering on the planks.

He exchanged the Colt for his hat, placed the first on the counter and the latter on his head. "Coming from you, I'm much obliged." He touched the brim, and strode out, leaving the barflies to their miserable solitude.

17

A Bird Without Restraint

THE NARROW ROAD CLIMBED higher, turned, and switched back, like a snake twining up the hillside. Soothing scents of eucalyptus and pine mingled with those of earth. Riot strolled beneath a shaded path of branch and vine. Birds whispered in the leaves and a lone cat watched his labored progress. After a month on a steamer, his muscles protested every uphill step. His heart was galloping, but his mind relished the exertion.

The Amsel mansion appeared and vanished through gaps in the trees. The house, caught somewhere between Gothic revival and hunting lodge, sat on a hill, tucked in a nook, safe in Nature's embrace. And beyond the Amsel home, higher on the hill, a cypress grove crowned the ridge, tall and imposing.

As Riot passed beneath an overgrown stone arch, he

wondered what it would have been like to grow up in two such disparate worlds. One of untamed wilderness and another of civilized society. Would a child adapt equally to both, or would she turn her back on one or the other? And what of Isobel Saavedra Amsel Kingston—which environment did she prefer?

The trail ended at a long succession of hewn stone steps. Riot stopped at the base to catch his breath. Rows of grapevines climbed with the steps, unhindered by the steep hillside. He pushed the brim of his hat back, and gazed up at the Amsel home. Verandas and windows wrapped around its contours, offering ample views of the surrounding countryside. He turned towards Richardson's Bay, and the breath in his throat caught.

Tiny ships with white sails flew across a sheet of crystal, weaving between rising islands and impossible shorelines. San Francisco sparkled in the mesmerizing distance—small and manageable to the eyes.

'Like a bird without restraint,' the breeze whispered through the leaves.

That bird, he thought, would never touch ground.

Riot would have liked to linger longer, but it was impossible to savor the vista when a woman's life rested heavily on his shoulders.

✥

The front door appeared to have been salvaged from a Spanish mission. Its dark oak and iron fittings were more suited to withstanding a battering ram than the knob of Riot's walking stick. His knock was answered with alacrity.

A Chinese man in silk tunic and loose trousers opened the door. He bowed, his long queue slipping over his shoulder. Silver hair was woven with black. And the lines on his proud face spoke of a long life.

Riot returned the bow and greeted the servant in his native tongue. The man's brow twitched with surprise.

"No visitors today."

Riot produced his card. "Mr. Amsel is not expecting me, but I'm sure he'll speak with me. I'm with Ravenwood Agency."

The servant alternately scrutinized the card and the man on his employer's doorstep. After a moment, the servant closed the door in Riot's face. A heavy latch rattled on the other side of the wood.

A protective sort of fellow, Riot surmised. Not a bad trait in a family servant.

The chirping of birds and rustling of leaves kept Riot company. In short order, the door was thrown open, and a tall older man grasped Riot's hand. Despite the sparse white hair dusting his head and the lines etching his face, his hand shake was firm and hearty. He wore a wool sweater over his shirt and tie rather than dressing gown and waistcoat.

"Have you found my Isobel, *Herr* Riot?" Marcus Amsel's blue eyes were bright and hopeful.

"No news, I'm afraid," Riot said, removing his hat. "I arrived in San Francisco only yesterday and am assisting Detective Smith in the search for your daughter."

A shadow dimmed hope. In an instant, Amsel aged decades. His lanky back stooped, and seventy some years weighed on his shoulders. "Yes, of course," he rallied. "Please, forgive Mr. Hop's rudeness. We have had police and press calling every day since the ransom demand was printed in the newspapers."

"Understandable." Riot handed Hop his hat, coat, and

stick with a nod. He surveyed the foyer, appreciating the rough wood and exposed rafters. The spartan decor was soothing.

"I appreciate your help," Amsel assured. "I know your reputation through the papers. You and your partner were involved in some bad business with the Tongs three years ago, if I recall correctly."

Hop's dark eyes flickered over to the detective, and Riot paused, meeting the servant's gaze. "Yes," he answered slowly, "we were."

Riot was led down a wide hallway. It opened into spacious common rooms that brought to mind a hacienda. Simple, sparse, yet elegant.

Amsel showed Riot to his study. Oak and leather, and thousands of books. Three full walls of stiff bindings that grudgingly made room for two doors and a fireplace. The fourth wall was devoted to a series of windows and french doors that opened onto a veranda. The world lay at their feet, vast and unending.

"Beautiful, isn't it?" Amsel's voice broke Riot's appreciation.

"With a view like this, I doubt I'd ever finish a thing."

Amsel smiled, and stood at his shoulder, towering despite the stoop in his back. "This was Isobel's favorite place." He gestured towards a padded bench by the windowsill, piled with cushions and books. "That is, when she was not roaming God only knows where. I hope we will have her back home tonight. The money is all here just as Isobel's abductors asked."

Amsel's gaze slid to a section of shelves.

"We were very careful, *Herr* Riot. As your Detective Smith advised, we told no one, not even the police. I know nothing of the second demand. It makes no sense."

Riot cleared his throat, settled into a leather armchair, and focused his thoughts. "What of your sons and their families?"

The tall man paced a worn trail across his study. "Yes, some of my sons and their wives know, but only because they were here when my grandson found the note on the doorstep. It was Christmas; our family was spending it together."

"All of your sons?"

In answer, Amsel plucked a framed photograph from its perch on the fireplace mantel. A large family stared out from the glass, cramped but cheerful in the confines of the frame. Two adults stood behind eleven children, one being Marcus Amsel with slightly more hair, and his wife, Catarina Amsel. Although she did not reach her husband's shoulder, her presence radiated from the photograph.

"This was taken ten years ago." It was clear Mr. Amsel had every intention of showing off his family, and Riot obliged, memorizing names and faces.

"Here is Aubert, our oldest; he manages the winery in Napa. And my dear Liliana, my wife's pride and joy—" The sting of grief was gone, but its echo was still present in the older man's voice. "Liliana was with child in this photograph. She died in childbirth, as did the infant." The photograph trembled, and Mr. Amsel focused on the second son. "Curtis is an engineer—he lives in the city. I'm afraid Decker was lost at sea five years ago. And Emmett manages the shipyards." All three men were as tall, strapping, and blond as their father had likely been in his youth.

"And here is Fernando. He is an archaeologist in Egypt." A dark and rakish man. "This is Gregor," Amsel beamed with pride. "Such a fine sailor that he was given captaincy of a steamer. He is only thirty-two. And here is

Vicilia, an extraordinary boatbuilder. The next is Merrik—he is in the army, stationed in the Philippines," Amsel confided with obvious distaste. His long finger hovered over the next son. Riot estimated the boy to be about ten. He had his mother's fine cheekbones and tanned complexion, but his father's light hair—in short, the boy was beautiful, as was his twin sister, who was standing at his side. "And Lotario, Isobel's twin brother. I do not know where he lives," Amsel said in clipped tones.

"No idea?"

Reluctantly, Amsel supplied more information. "Somewhere in San Francisco. He is in the theatre, an entertainer. I taught him to build boats, to sail, I paid for university abroad, and yet he is a lay about. We do not speak of him, but he and Isobel were once close." The father moved on to the eleventh child, eyes dimming with sadness. "And here is my Isobel."

Ten year old Isobel resembled Lotario in every way, save for her expression and attire. Whereas the brother was clearly enjoying the camera's attention, she positively seethed. The little girl wore a frilly white dress, her arms were crossed and her feet were bare. She looked as if she'd like to bite off the photographer's head.

Amsel smiled at Riot's amusement. "Isobel wanted to be just like her brothers. Let children be children, I say, but her mother stuffed her in that dress for the family portrait."

"I'm sure she is delightful," Riot replied, politely. "Who was present when the ransom demand was discovered?"

"Curtis and Vicilia, along with their families. This home has always been bursting with activity, *Herr* Riot. When the children were young, my wife and I would shove them out of the house. 'Go play, leave us in peace,' we would say, but now, it is nice to have a noisy home again."

"Were you expecting Isobel?"

"We were hopeful," he confided. "But she was newly married. Alex has his own life."

"Were you pleased when your daughter married Alex Kingston?" Riot asked, bluntly.

Amsel sighed. He returned the photograph to its place of honor, adjusting it absentmindedly. At length he spoke, "Last year was very bad for business. Both the winery in Napa and the shipyards were plagued with disasters. A fire, another bad grape harvest, failed lumber negotiations, contracts retracted—my wife thought us cursed. And then there was Isobel."

"Her abduction, you mean?"

Amsel hesitated. "Before."

Marcus Amsel carried a secret, and the father was weighing the wisdom of confiding in a stranger. He just needed a little nudge.

"Mr. Amsel," Riot said, softly. "I am sure you are aware of my agency's reputation. We—" He stumbled over the word, quickly correcting his mistake, "I am discreet, in all matters. Whatever you say here will remain with me."

Amsel inhaled and then exhaled, turning to face Riot. He clasped his hands behind his back. "If Liliana was my wife's pride and joy, then Isobel is surely mine. I indulged my daughter, *Herr* Riot. She was like a bird, as beautiful and spirited as her mother. I could not cage such beauty. Unfortunately, little girls grow up into young women. And young women have reputations."

A soft knock heralded the arrival of tea. Hop entered with a tray, set it on the table, and set about pouring two cups with meticulous, yet swift, ceremony.

"*Danke*, Hop." Amsel nodded as he accepted the offered cup. Hop bowed and shuffled out as silently as he had entered. Amsel settled his long body into the armchair next to Riot's. Both chairs faced the window to better appreciate the view. Riot sipped his tea, allowing time for Amsel to gather his thoughts.

"As a child, Isobel was prone to roam," Amsel began. "She followed her brothers everywhere, even when they did not wish her to. And then she began to wander alone, disappearing for entire days, evading her brothers when I tasked them with watching her. At night, she would climb out of her window and walk the hills, exploring, trespassing in the old mine tunnels—everywhere she wasn't allowed." Amsel clucked his tongue, eyes drifting in supplication to the rafters. "A parent can only worry so much.

"If that were not enough, she began sailing the bay, docking in San Francisco, and wandering the city. It was too much. If it had not been for Curtis, her name would have been dragged through the newspapers. We had no choice." Amsel sighed heavily with regret. "We sent her to a young ladies school in Dresden in the company of a chaperone. We hoped that distance from her home would calm her down.

"To our shock and joy, Isobel flourished on the continent. She abided the rules and dutifully studied, graduating with high honors. Shortly after, Catarina and I received a letter from Isobel's chaperone. The two of them wished to travel the continent. We agreed, increasing Isobel's allowance. For two years, we received regular correspondence. All seemed well."

Amsel paused, taking a long, fortifying sip of his tea. "Early this year, I received a wire from a friend who was traveling, stating that he had seen Isobel alone on a steamer. She claimed that her chaperone had fallen ill and was laid up in the cabin. Concerned, I sent Fernando a wire, asking that he find his sister, to check on her well-being.

"Fernando finally found her in Venice," Amsel said, harshly. "The chaperone had abandoned my daughter two years before, and Isobel had pretended all that time that the woman was still with her. She was, *Herr* Riot, living in the home of two young men, a fencer and an artist. Pah!"

"An unpleasant surprise, no doubt," Riot murmured, hiding his bemusement behind a sip of tea.

"Fernando dragged her home and Curtis managed to keep the newspapers silent yet again. It is a wonder she was not with child. So, yes, Catarina and I were surprised —but relieved—when she met Alex Kingston and agreed to marry him before rumor had ruined her reputation."

"But she didn't marry him straight away?"

"They were introduced over the summer. She enrolled at university, and then a few months later, suddenly announced her engagement. Young women, who can know what goes on in their minds?" Amsel gestured dismissively. His daughter had given him a lifetime of grief; he was simply happy to see her settled. Conversely, Riot was highly suspicious.

"Was Kingston aware of your daughter's precarious reputation?"

The question startled Amsel. "I do not know," he began slowly, setting his teacup on its saucer with a rattle. "It was not a good time for our family. When Isobel left for Europe, she was fifteen. Four years later, when she returned, she was a grown woman—a stranger to me. There was little time to reacquaint ourselves. Even now, I have not told my children the extent of our losses."

"And the ransom money?"

"I sold a property in Napa. A vineyard," Amsel confided, hoarsely, like a man who had given away his firstborn. "The rest was a loan from the bank. There is no money left that is not already spent or tied up in equity, *Herr* Riot."

"You were able to sell a property in a week's time?"

"The buyer had made numerous offers before. That is how I met Alex."

"Who was the buyer?"

"Thomas Wade, an investor and developer who is working on a railway line from Vallejo to Calistoga."

"Did Mr. Wade ever threaten or pressure you to sell?"

Amsel shook his head. "He was disappointed—persistent as men like him are, but civil."

"How were you planning on paying for your daughter's university?"

"My wife received a sizable inheritance," Amsel explained. "As the only child of the Saavedra line, her father put his fortune in a trust, so whether or not she married, it would always remain her money. I have honored that arrangement. And Catarina has made the same arrangement for Isobel. Upon my wife's death—God forbid—the estate will pass to Isobel one day."

Brisk footsteps stormed the hallway, and the study door opened without ceremony. Both men were startled from their armchairs. A formidable woman, not owing to height but presence, stood in its frame. Her hair was steel rather than worn, coiled in a severe bun that highlighted her high cheekbones and bronzed skin. Stormy eyes swept over Riot.

"Have you found my daughter?" A strong hand clutched a thick, carved cane.

Amsel hastily stepped next to his wife. "Atticus Riot,

this is my dear wife, Catarina."

"An honor, Mrs. Amsel." Riot bowed. "To answer your question: no."

"Why aren't you looking for her, *Senhor* Riot?"

"I had some questions for your husband."

"Questions will not bring my daughter home."

"But the answers may lead us to her."

Mrs. Amsel bristled at his easy assurance. She stiffened, turned to her husband, and words flew from her lips. While Riot wasn't fluent in Portuguese, it was not dissimilar to Spanish. He caught a few familiar words and a strong sense that Mrs. Amsel did not hold Detective Smith in high regard—nor, it seemed, Riot.

Amsel replied in sharp Germanic tones. A flurry of words flew between the couple in their respective tongues. Although Riot was fluent in German, the exchange was too cryptic to follow, more gesture than substance.

Abruptly, Mrs. Amsel turned on Riot. "My daughter's history is none of your concern."

"Her future *is* my concern, Mrs. Amsel," Riot replied smoothly. "And to be blunt, I fear she doesn't have much time."

His words hit the couple like a brick. Amsel gripped his wife's shoulder, and she placed a hand over his.

"Old Sue is dead," Riot explained. "It may be unrelated, but I'm not one for coincidences. I think the men who paid her to deliver the ransom note wanted to cover their tracks."

"But I have the money here—all of it," Amsel protested frantically. "Surely they wouldn't kill Isobel!"

"I can't be certain, but if I'm to find her, then I'll need a better place to start than every boat and port in San Francisco bay."

Mrs. Amsel raised her chin. "Ask your questions."

18

The Gossip

THE SUN BEAT ON his fedora. Riot leaned on a saloon post, his back to the bay, gazing up the steep hillside. Tiers of class climbed ever higher. The finest homes perched on top like regal lords fighting for dominance.

It was a long way for an old woman to walk. Surely someone would have seen Old Sue deliver the ransom demand to the Amsel house, even at night.

Riot fished a knitted cap out of his pocket. It was the half-finished project from Old Sue's shanty. He supported the cap with his fingertips, estimating the size. Old Sue had been a small woman, but the cap didn't strike him as a hat intended for a woman. There were no frills, no embellishments—just a simple, navy blue yarn. The kind you might expect to find on a sailor.

Too small for a man.

Riot looked towards the Amsel residence, following the long snaking road with his eyes. An old woman, who couldn't carry ten empty bottles, wouldn't walk up that path, especially at night.

The knit cap suddenly slid neatly into the puzzle.

'*Yes, of course,*' breathed Ravenwood over Riot's shoulder. Another phantom joined the owlish man. A bent, little woman, shuffled from one pool of light to the next, fading in and out of his thoughts.

If the bartender at the blind pig was to be believed, then the men hadn't paid Old Sue with bottles, as she had told Tim, but with coin.

'*Obviously,*' Ravenwood grunted. Riot imagined his mentor's brows drawing together in disapproval.

"I'm as daft as a mule," agreed Riot. Drunks didn't count pennies; they counted booze. When Old Sue had told Tim that she was paid two bottles of gin, she had in fact been paid fifty cents to deliver the ransom note—not enough for her preferred gin, but enough for two boot-legged bottles full of God-awful drink that could lay a mule flat. And why walk down Water Street, when the blind pig was so close to home?

Therefore, Old Sue had encountered Mrs. Kingston's abductors at the docks—where it was common for ma-riners to offer her supplies and allow her to mend nets. With all the faces she encountered during her day, she likely didn't remember the men, only the coin for gin, which meant that Tim had been asking the wrong ques-tions. He had been asking if anyone had seen someone give Old Sue two bottles. And of course they hadn't, be-cause she had been paid with coins.

Riot walked down Water Street, dodging wagons, gamblers, and fishermen. His thoughts sped forward, reassembling events as he approached the telegraph office.

A robust woman, sturdy and round, was sweeping the porch. Green eyes traveled over his gentlemanly attire, and then she smiled at his patient gaze.

"Pardon me, ma'am." He tipped his hat. "I have a message that wants delivering. Does your office employ a messenger?"

"Not in an official capacity, but the boys are always eager for work," she answered, nodding towards a wide alley, where sounds of playing children erupted onto the street.

"Are they trustworthy?"

"Surely for a penny." She smiled. "Shall I call them?" Her eyes shifted to a bell on the porch.

"No need. A pleasant day to you, ma'am." The woman blushed at his manner.

Riot caught himself before leaving. "May I ask a question?"

"Happy to answer if I can."

"Do you know Old Sue?"

"That I do, but then everyone in town knows the old gal."

"Were any of the children in the habit of helping her?"

Her smile fell. Suspicion replaced amiability. "Are you with the press?"

"Certainly not." He produced his card. "Atticus Riot, with Ravenwood Agency. I'm afraid Old Sue has been murdered."

"Murdered?" Her lips thinned. Shock cooled her rosy cheeks. "Who'd want to murder the harmless dear?"

"I'm attempting to ascertain the answer to that very question. Was she well thought of in town?"

"I wouldn't say that, exactly." The woman frowned.

"She was well into the ruin, but she was a fixture in our town—like a stubborn stump in the middle of the road. Now that you mention it, I haven't seen her in days."

"When I went to her home, I found a cap that she had begun knitting—smallish, navy blue. Have you any idea who she was making it for?"

"She was a dear when she was sober. Wouldn't hurt a fly. She had a rough life, but always had a soft spot for children as destitute as herself. I think—" The woman clicked her teeth together, abruptly swallowing her words.

Riot waited patiently. Silence always wanted to be filled. And his eyes, deep and knowing, cleared the way for words to pour into the gap, releasing a torrent.

"Well, it's just that she wasn't always old. Earned her living in ways I won't speak of, or so I was told. I think her donating as she does—did, was penance for a life of sin."

"Were the children fond of her?"

"I wouldn't say fond, but she always had a tune on her lips." The woman chuckled. "Probably more bawdy than was Christian, but she'd give them little gifts: gloves, hats, small treats. Harmless she was, not like all the wild folks pouring in from the city, gambling, drinking, brawling in the streets. We're one step away from the Barbary Coast, is what I always say."

"Surely not that bad?"

"You've heard about the Amsel girl who's been abducted, I'm sure."

"Are you referring to Mrs. Kingston of San Francisco?"

"Formally Amsel," the woman corrected. "Born and raised here, and she'll always be an Amsel in my mind. Known her since she was a babe."

"No doubt she is a charming young lady."

The woman snorted and swept imaginary dirt off one plank. "Miss Isobel? Before her parents were gifted with sense and sent her off to one of them fancy European schools for ladies, you couldn't hardly tell her apart from her brothers." The woman's tone was disapproving but her eyes gleamed with pride. "San Francisco had their Lillie Hitchcock, but we had our Isobel. I always hoped she would marry and settle down, but I didn't reckon she'd marry the likes of Kingston."

"He's not well regarded in Sausalito?"

It was the wrong question. The woman's hands tightened around her broom handle. She pressed her lips together, sealing them like a clam.

"I have work to attend to, Mr. Riot. I've lingered long enough."

"Thank you for your time, ma'am." Riot touched his fingers to the brim of his hat. As he stepped off the porch, he paused, glancing at a sign in the window that proclaimed the telegraph's support of the *Municipal Improvement Club.*

The woman had said far more than she knew.

19

A Dubious Umpire

THE EARTH HELD ITS breath and the gulls swallowed their
cries. Stubby fingers stretched over an orb of cork, leather,
and yarn. The ball held the power to shatter the world. All
eyes were glued on the mythical orb.

An arm reached back, gathering courage and force,
and then hurled the missile, letting it fly. Hope and dreams
spun towards the batter.

A *Crack!* fractured the field. Screams, bare feet, and
hurried screeching washed over the lone witness to determination. The right fielder ran, leapt, stretching out a
battered mitt, and fell in a puff of dust, emerging a split
second later to scramble after his failed catch.

The hitter ran for his life. A streak of white flew towards home base. The runner slid, the catcher reached,
and *Safe!* was abruptly called. Two pint-sized players leapt

up, hurling insults at one another. In a cloud of dust, two teams converged, disintegrating into a mob of shouts.

"He was out!"

"Safe!"

"Too late."

"Was a foot away!"

The smallest, and loudest, tore off his cap, slamming it onto the field. His red face heated to dangerous levels. Before the tea kettle could explode, Riot stepped forward.

"I had a fair vantage point of the play." Ten sets of eyes locked onto the stranger. The children were a sea of mismatched faces, a motley assortment of color, but all equally hopeful.

"Well, was he safe or was he out?" the smallest demanded, stepping in front of his gang. He hooked his fingers in his pockets and tilted his head back to look Riot square in the eyes. The boy resembled a puffed-up rooster. Given his compact frame and confidence, he had all the makings of a regular freckled scrapper.

Riot looked from one smudged face to the next, allowing tension to build and silence to settle on the field.

"I have some business with you gentlemen. I propose an exchange of information."

"Information?" the Rooster's interest was piqued.

"Just tell us, mister," a plaintive cry rippled through the group. Riot held up a calming hand, quieting the restless natives.

"Shall we consider it a gentleman's agreement?" he asked their leader.

"Deal." The Rooster spit on his hand and extended it. Riot sealed their agreement with spit of his own. The Rooster frowned at the bespectacled gentleman. Most adults didn't return the honest gesture. Man and boy sealed the deal, one with bemusement and the other with a wrinkled nose. The Rooster quickly wiped his hand on his grubby pants, eliciting a giggle from the sea of astonished faces.

"Might any of you know Old Sue?" Riot inquired, getting right down to business.

The children glanced at each other, all equally puzzled.

"Sure we know her," said their leader.

"Have you seen her of late?"

As one, they shrugged.

"Did one of you, or one of your friends, run an errand for her in the last week?"

The Rooster crossed his arms. "You don't look like a patrolman. And you're too slick for the press. You a Pinkerton?"

'Observant for an eight year old,' Ravenwood rasped on the wind. Riot silently agreed with the voice, and answered the little man, "I'm an *ex*-Pinkerton."

"Did you get tossed?" a chubby face asked.

"I didn't abide by their strike-breaking tactics." A murmur of agreement and instant respect traveled through the collective.

"Do you know Old King Brady?" a cherub's voice rose from the chorus.

"I have not met the Bradys," Riot answered simply. Informing the group that the dime novel heroes were as fictional as *Pluck and Luck* would not loosen any tongues. "However, I have met Mr. Sherlock Holmes."

Their eyes widened. "Are you an Irregular?"

"No, I'm with Ravenwood Detective Agency." Disappointment rippled across their faces. Riot was no Watson, and certainly no biographer. Ravenwood's cases never made it past the newspapers.

'*And they never would have made it that far if I'd had my way,*' Ravenwood grumbled in his ear. Riot pushed the voice out of his mind. "Back to my question."

"Is Old Sue in some sort of trouble?" a voice asked from the multitude.

"Cross-questioning was not part of our agreement, gentlemen."

Ten faces waited. Riot stood firm against their collective silence, leaning casually on his walking stick as if he had all the time in the world.

Finally, the Rooster gestured his gang into a huddle. Hushed voices hissed in argument, ebbing from one side to the next, until a stick of a child was shoved out of the circle. The boy paled and tried to retreat.

"Tell 'im, Eliza," the Rooster urged. Riot mentally corrected his assumption—the stick-like child was a girl.

"Miss Eliza." Riot tipped his hat politely, and crouched down to her level. "Atticus Riot. A pleasure to meet you."

The girl looked back to the Rooster.

"Just spit it out. The man doesn't care you were out when you weren't supposed to be."

The girl finally worked up the nerve to answer, and when she started, there was no damming the rush of lisping words.

"Old Sue paid me a penny to run a letter up to the Amsel's and I put it on the front porch just like she said, knocked and ran, and to prove I done it I snatched a handful of grapes from the Amsel's vines, just like Old Sue said to do." Full stop. Large inhale, and a mighty expansion of ribs.

"What day was this, Miss Eliza?"

"Day after Christmas."

"What time?"

"It was dark." The girl shrugged, and added, "After dinner."

"Was anyone with Old Sue?"

Hesitation. "No, mister."

"What about when you returned with the grapes?"

"No, mister."

Riot regarded the girl. Under his steady gaze, she began to fidget. The edge of his lips twitched upwards in encouragement. The girl relented.

"That's to say I followed her down to Whaler's Cove. It was high tide. The boats were up in the water."

"That would have been around eight o'clock in the evening, then?"

"I suppose." Eliza shrugged.

"What did you see?"

"Old Sue met a man over by the *Walhalla*. I'm not supposed to be near there."

"Did you see the man?"

"It was dark."

"Was he tall?"

"Maybe."

"Taller than me?" Riot stood so she would have something to compare.

Eliza wrinkled her nose. "You ain't that big, mister."

"I'm afraid not." Riot chuckled, fastidiously adjusting his spectacles.

"The man looked like any other sailor."

"Big shoulders, then?"

Eliza nodded. "And a coat and a cap."

"Miss Eliza," Riot said softly, lowering himself to her level once again. "I need you to think real hard. This is very important. Did you notice anything, no matter how small, about the man Old Sue spoke with? Maybe his voice, the way he walked, the way he stood?"

"I've told you all I know about the man."

Riot sighed. "Did this man see you, Miss Eliza?"

"No, sir, not even when I snuck on the dock and followed him down to his boat."

Riot blinked. Clearing the surprise from his throat, he asked, "You saw his boat?"

"You didn't ask me about that."

"How careless of me."

'*Idiotic would be my word of choice*,' the voice from the past corrected.

"The boat was a single-mast trawler."

"You like boats, then?"

"I do." The girl nodded happily.

"Did the boat have a name?" Eliza couldn't have been more than six, but considering his earlier lapse, he had to make an attempt.

"I can't read." She scratched her head. "But there was a *M* and an *A*—" Riot held his breath, lest he break the girl's concentration. "And maybe a *P*." Eliza shrugged.

"Do you remember the slip where the boat was moored?"

"The fourth down."

"Thank you, Miss Eliza." Riot gave the little girl a rare smile. Eliza smiled back, displaying her two missing front teeth.

"Are you sure the man didn't see you?"

"Why?" the Rooster asked. "Is he trouble?"

"The man in question is a bad sort," Riot explained. "I'll inform your parents."

"No!" The Rooster stepped in front of Eliza, and the girl paled. "Her old man will knock her about something fierce."

'*A naive overreaction, nothing more,*' Ravenwood announced pompously. '*Spare the rod and spoil the child.*' Riot shoved the memory aside, smoothing his beard in consideration.

"Listen to me, all of you," he said gravely. "No one, and I mean no one can know Eliza saw that man. If anyone comes asking after that letter—none of you knows a thing. Understood?"

Ten heads bobbed.

"Not even the police," Riot said for good measure. This new development made him uneasy. "Will you swear?" He raised his hand and ten hands followed suit with varying degrees of determination.

"I swear," they murmured.

"Miss Eliza," he said, firmly. "For your own safety, I want you to stay with this group, don't wander off alone. Can you all remain together when you're not at home?"

"Sure we can," said the Rooster.

"If you need anything, here is my card." The Rooster scrutinized the print. The others crowded close to get a look of their own.

"What's this bird on there?"

"A raven."

"If your name is Riot, then why's a raven on it?"

"I was Ravenwood's partner."

'*You'll be here all day at this rate,*' a voice murmured.

"How come—"

Riot held up his hand. "Would you like to know if your batter was safe or out?"

Ten children stood alert.

Riot let the tension build until they were practically bursting with curiosity.

"Safe," he pronounced distinctly.

The pack erupted with triumphant shouts from half

and protests from the other. In the tumult of arguing and jeers, Riot slipped away lest the offended team decide to call his judgment into question. After all, he hadn't actually been in a position to see home base.

20

Call to Arms

DARKNESS WAS COMPLETE. THE hold swayed, salt water sloshed back and forth, splashing on her crude pallet. Open water. Isobel shifted, and groaned, working jaw muscles that were newly freed. It seemed it no longer mattered if she screamed. However, her wrists and ankles remained tied. Her coat had been removed.

Gingerly, Isobel shimmied herself into a sitting position, slumping heavily against the rough hull. The smell of blood permeated her senses. Hair stuck to the side of her face, crusted and dry. Her skull continued to throb. Was it day or night? How long had she been unconscious? Where was she going?

Nowhere she wished to go.

The single answer chased away the other questions. All useless, given her present situation. The men would kill her here or there, now or later, and if that wasn't their intent, then they'd keep her alive. But for what, precisely?

Isobel had never much cared for waiting. And she had no intention of doing so now. She lay down on the lumpy sacks, twisting and moving, working wrists and arms, flexing her numb fingers in the confines of thick ropes.

Luck, God, or unprofessionalism had kept her abductors from removing her gloves. She silently thanked all three, and then cursed her corset and its stiff confines. Twice, she was forced to pause and catch her breath, heaving in the darkness, willing air into her constricted lungs. The struggle would have been impossible in a proper corset.

Millimeter by millimeter, the rope loosened. She shimmied and stretched, shifting knuckles and joints, until a hand slipped free of its glove.

Isobel gasped with relief. Her body trembled and her teeth chattered. Whether it was with fear, cold, or exhilaration, she did not know, but she moved quickly, acting on instinct before doubt could take root in her bones. Slipping free of the rope, she turned to her ankles, working at the knots with numb fingers. With the last knot unwound, she brushed the ropes to the side as if they were living things seeking to entrap her again.

The darkness was no longer absolute. Her eyes and body were acclimating to her prison. She climbed to her feet, swaying with the hold. Slowly, arm out, hand brushing the bulkhead, she shuffled forward, taking stock of her surroundings. There wasn't much.

A ladder stopped at the hatch, whispering of freedom.

An inch of salt water gathered in the middle of the hull and her hat sat on the floor, as battered and soaked as she felt.

Hopeful, she rummaged through an old crate. It contained rotted boots and rusted tacks, probably surplus from the booming days of the Gold Rush. At the start of the boom, tacks were worth their weight in gold and boots were near to priceless. An empty bucket sat near the ladder, along with frayed nets, sailcloth, and three rotting fish.

Isobel frowned at her sparse inventory. And then she smirked.

Worth their weight in gold.

Sparing a single glance for the hatch, Isobel moved back to the pallet. She sat down, unlaced her impractical shoes, unhooked wool stockings from their garters, and stood. She reached into the crate, gathering a handful of tacks from its bottom and poured them into her stocking, until a fist-sized ball of rusty metal lay in its toe.

With her prize in hand, she returned to her pallet and settled down, carefully wrapping the leg of the stocking around its toe. She grabbed the discarded bindings, and moved through familiar motions, tying a Monkey's Fist, a knot she had learned before she could read. This time she wove the knot around a fist of metal, creating a slung shot.

Every sailor worth his salt could tie a Monkey's Fist blindfolded. The weighted end was useful for moor lines— and as a weapon. Slung shots were a favorite on the Barbary Coast. Easy to fashion, and deadly accurate. In skilled hands, the heavy fist at the end of a three foot length of rope made for a formidable weapon.

Isobel shed her cumbersome garments, breathing freely when her ribcage was released from the corset's grip.

Gutting the pallet's innards, she transferred the straw to her corset and dress. Standing in chemise and bloomers, the cold cut straight through to her bones. She pushed discomfort aside, plucked the hat pin from its plumage and slid the eager tip through her garter. The hat pin wouldn't kill a man, but it would definitely blind.

Satisfied with her growing arsenal, she turned to the crate, rummaging through the boots until she found a pair with the soles intact. A cut on the sole of her foot from a nail or splinter of glass would not help her now. Donning her new footwear, she picked up her corset and began worrying at the fabric with a tack, plucking thread after thread. When the fabric split, she inserted her fingers and yanked out the metal stay with vicious satisfaction.

Footsteps thudded overhead. Isobel paused, reaching for the slung shot. A tense second later, the footsteps receded, leaving the wash of waves.

Grabbing her fashionably heeled shoe, she overturned the bucket, placed the end of the steel stay on top and pressed the narrow heel over steel. Holding one end of the stay in place, she bent the thin metal up and down, creating a diagonal crease. When the metal snapped, she repeated the process, creating a jagged, uneven end with a decent point. Using the laces from her shoes, she wrapped the cord around the sharpened stay, creating a tidy little shiv.

Isobel slipped the shiv through her garter, tossed her shoes into the crate, and focused on restoring order to her hair. With deft fingers, she plaited the mass, cinched the end with shoe lace, and turned to fluff her straw twin.

Satisfied with her efforts, she kicked the bucket over, letting it bang against the wood, picked up her slung shot and moved to the ladder, pressing herself under its slope.

Heart racing, head pounding, she waited.

21

The Magpie

THREE OLD MEN SAT on overturned crates, reminiscing about better days—more plentiful fish, calmer seas, and sturdier sailors. Their pipes were lit, and the smoke warred with the day, chasing away the sun with masculine careless-ness.

Of the trio, Tim made up the third. Having no desire to join the conversation, Riot caught his eye and kept walking. Tim could talk the ear off a sloth and was just as slow to untangle himself from a conversation. While Tim continued to smoke and converse, Riot settled himself at a cafe table, alternately sipping his tea and eating a sandwich while he watched the sails glide across Richardson's Bay.

It took twenty minutes for Tim to extract himself from

what was sure to be either old acquaintances or a pair who would one day prove to be. A strong cloud of sweet tobacco signaled Tim's arrival, a moment before the man plopped himself onto the chair opposite. He took one look at Riot's lunch, frowned, and turned to the waitress to order a plate of steak and potatoes, and a strong coffee.

"I haven't seen Nabs and Humphrey since my crabbing days," Tim said, by way of introduction.

"How long did your crabbing endeavors last?"

"Two days."

Riot chuckled, and somewhere from the shadows Ravenwood harrumphed. Ignoring the persistent presence, Riot set down his tea, leaned back, and crossed his legs.

"There is a small local girl by the name of Eliza: six by my estimation, brown-haired, freckles, two missing front teeth. She tucks her braids under her cap and looks like the rest of the pack. I need you to put a discreet guard on her."

Tim raised his bushy brows. Riot filled him in on the day's activities, and by the end of his narrative, Tim was grinning from ear to ear, appearing somewhere between impish and deranged.

"*M* and an *A* and a *P* you say?"

"So my informant informed."

"It just so happens that while you were ingratiating yourself with the local bootlegger, I was having a pleasant sort of conversation. Nabs and Humphrey plant their leathery hides on their chairs every day to watch the tides ebb. They were able to identify a number of boats that the ferry crew recalled, but more importantly, Nabs aired his irritation over the current stock of lazy mariners infesting his waterways. This little tale of his involved a trawler christened the *Magpie*."

Riot reached for his stick, where it rested against his

chair. As Tim continued, he unconsciously traced the silver knob.

"The trawler, they say, arrived at the cove with the morning high tide—that'd be 6:30 on the 26th. The captain set his boat on the big timbers on shore, and at low tide set about scraping her hull. Nabs and Humphrey didn't much care for the captain's method or the state of his trawler. And here is where it gets interesting."

Tim leaned over his plate in a conspiratorial manner. "At 9:45ish, two men pulled up in a wagon, hoisted a new sail to their shoulders, and delivered it to the *Magpie*. The reason Nabs and Humphrey took note was that, in their esteemed opinion, the sail the trawler had was the only maintained part of the boat. So why, they wondered, was her captain having a new one delivered?"

"Did the delivery men leave?"

"One remained, and the other drove off in the wagon, only to return fifteen minutes later. After we finish here, I'll see if I can track down the wagon."

"Did you get a description of these three men?"

"One largish, built like an ox, with a black beard. The other, the captain, had a square jaw, average build, and light hair. And the last was slim, *Irish* they said, because he cursed like the devil."

"A fine cover," Riot said with appreciation. "With hundreds of boats moored in Richardson's Bay on any given day, strangers are a common sight."

"That they are, but the captain wasn't unknown to Nabs and Humphrey."

Riot's fingers stilled.

"A scavenger, they said; comes and goes as he pleases."

"Does the captain have a regular port?"

"Unknown."

"I know someone who might know." If the captain was a Union member then Val the Weasel might recognize the *Magpie*, and if he wasn't, then Val would likely be outraged. Riot removed his spectacles and methodically cleaned the glass with a napkin. "Either way you toss the dice this business reeks of careful planning."

"Well, they skipped a cog somewhere along the line with that second ransom demand."

"Someone certainly did."

"Do you think they'll show tonight with Mrs. Kingston?"

Riot frowned. At length, he said, "I think we had better find Mrs. Kingston."

22

Counter Attack

FEAR AND COLD CREPT up her spine. Overturning the bucket was the only sound she was willing to risk. Anything more and her abductors would be on guard. So Isobel bided her time, distracting herself with a game of mental chess, only the pieces were real, moving and shifting, changing tactics and outwitting one another. In the end, she feared the Ivory King had won.

It took her abductors half the night to check on (or toy with) their victim. Thudding footsteps snapped her attention to the present. The hatch was peeled back with a creak of hinges. Gum-soled boots navigated the rungs with plodding effort.

Isobel pressed herself against the corner, willing herself to blend with the shadows, as lantern light bounced in the hold, searing flashes of an ugly square jaw and spidery veins into her mind.

The man reeked of rum.

"Let's see how yer fairin' in yer cozy home," a voice slurred. Her heart leapt, catching in her throat. She swallowed the thumping organ back down, tightening her fist around the slung shot.

The man's eyes were drawn to the pallet, lingering greedily on the prone shadow. "As the captain, I 'ave a right to acquaint myself with my passengers."

Isobel planted her foot, brought her arm up, and struck. Newton and his laws were set into motion. They ended with a crack. The man crumpled, the lantern shattered, and Isobel flew up the ladder.

"What now?" Rushing footsteps, moonlight, and an angry voice hovered above. She emerged on deck, bristling for a fight. Two men converged, one ox-like and one slim.

Isobel struck, catching the larger man square in his jaw with her slung shot. The blow whipped the man's face to the side, even as Slim attacked. His quick jab connected with her cheek. She staggered backwards, dropping to the deck. Slim advanced, and she hurled the weighted rope at his feet. The rope wound around his legs with a gleeful shake, wrapping tight and clinging, bringing Slim to his knees. She drew her shiv and plunged the jagged tip into his side.

Brutish power slammed into her back, driving her to the deck. The next blow rammed into her ribs, expelling air from her lungs. Pain narrowed her vision. Bulky arms wrapped around her waist. She squirmed and twisted in the powerful embrace, facing two pinpricks of fury. The gates of Hell dwelt in the man's eyes.

Isobel brought her knee up, stoking the fires. The Ox roared. His arms loosened a fraction, but not enough. She drew her hatpin and jabbed it into his eye.

The arms abandoned their prize.

The man screamed, swinging wildly, blindly. His rage bounded across the sea, and a shot rang out. Wood exploded by her ear. Without thought, she rushed towards the rail, and dove overboard as another shot rang in the night.

Ice welcomed her, blackness embraced, and Isobel Kingston vanished into the sea.

23

Beyond the Pale

A STIFF BREEZE WHIPPED through the Golden Gate. The fishing boat dipped and rose with a spray of salt. Atticus Riot twisted around, glancing back across the bay. Silver froth gathered on the distant hills, slowly rolling down the steep slopes, spilling into valleys and ravines. The Silver Mistress was stirring.

A snap of sails and shift of rigging brought him back around. He turned his attention on the approaching shore-line, moving aside as Younger secured a line. Stilted houses sat calmly in a horseshoe-shaped cove, and piers stretched into the water, where Chinese shrimping junks moored. The redwood boats were long and wide, and their sheer was low and close to the water. Perfect for navigating the shallows.

The hills above the village were steep. Grass swept up their slopes, interrupted by green shrubs and lone pines. Six miles of shoreline lay between the Chinese shrimping village and Ferry Point, a developing terminus for the Santa Fe Railway Company.

"I doubt an Irishman, a sandy-haired fellow, and a bearded ox would drop anchor at a Chinese shrimping village," Tim hollered over the wind. He was cold again, huddled in his peacoat, beard damp with sea spray, and looking thoroughly miserable.

Riot frowned at his old friend. For the first time since arriving, he was struck by how much Tim had aged in his absence. The thought hit Riot hard. He cleared his throat, recalled Tim's comment, and forced himself to answer.

"The village would hardly report any boats that kept to themselves."

"I don't much trust a man known as the Weasel."

The *Magpie* had been known to Val the Weasel. The Union man did not much care for non-unionized Scavengers, and the captain had been ignoring claims for years. The captain, Val had said, was a man of opportunity who went by the name of Long and operated alone.

"It's all we have at the moment," Riot replied. "Val didn't give me the names off the top of his head. He tracked down Captain Long's preferred ports through a grapevine of informants."

"Maybe he just wanted your money," Tim pointed out, scanning the shoreline.

"If you hadn't told me of the *Magpie* first, I would have suspected Val was setting his rival up for the gallows. The man didn't care for Captain Long one bit."

Unfortunately, finding an unremarkable trawler on a

bay of thousands was not a task suited for a single after-noon. Time was running out for Mrs. Kingston. At the very least, Val had narrowed down their search. While Tim's Vigilance boys were combing the docks along Fish-erman's Wharf, Riot had recruited the help of Red and Younger. The two fishermen were eager to volunteer their boat and expertise. Together, they had already searched the shoreline surrounding the *Giant Powder Company*, and they were now sailing towards Ferry Point.

Red navigated the shoreline swiftly, trimming sails and spilling wind whenever a trawler came into view. Riot pulled his brim low and squinted towards the Golden Gate and the falling sun. They were losing daylight.

Ferry Point came into view around a bend. The long stretch of land was being cleared for a railway that was aimed at the hills. While Riot scanned the shoreline, the crew's eyes were drawn to the peninsula's tip, where a maze of masts bobbed in a sheltered harbor.

A dark, jagged bore cut through the steep hillside. It was the beginnings of a tunnel for the Santa Fe Railway line. Up and over a mound, and farther down the shoreline, was a natural cove, overshadowed by oak and eucalyptus and clogged with driftwood and flotsam. A flock of angry seagulls fought over what looked like a pile of seaweed, wailing and crying with eagerness and a rush of feathers.

"Red," Riot shouted, pointing towards the beach. "Bring us in closer."

Younger spilled the wind, the sail luffed with a snap, and the boat slowed, drifting into the cove. The men's eyes were now fixed on the mound of seaweed. With numb fingers, Riot fished a piece of drift wood from the water, and hurled it towards the gulls. The flock dispersed with piercing screams, catching wind for a split second, before diving back to their prize.

The break in feathers was enough. A shock of pale hair and paler skin mingled with the sea and sand.

✣

The big man, all black beard and hardened skin, was brought to his knees, retching in a tangle of roots. Red kept a respectful distance, hat in hand, murmuring last rites for the dead. His old eyes had seen death aplenty, but a man never got used to seeing violence done to one so young.

Tim was helping Riot clear away the seaweed. Flies, beetles, and crabs swarmed over sickly flesh, crawling beneath the tattered remains of a green wool dress. Riot brushed the dingy hair from the corpse's face, revealing an inhuman visage. There were no lids to close, or even eyes to cover. The gulls had picked the body clean.

The body was bruised and battered, the clothing torn. Riot slipped on his gloves and bent over the remains, shifting torn fabric, and taking stock of the bruising.

"She was used badly," Riot stated, grimly. "But no killing wound. I'd wager she was drowned. Red, Younger, can you identify this woman?"

"Hard to tell," Red frowned. "I knew Isobel for the life in her eyes."

"Appears so," Younger rasped, and quickly glanced away.

"The dress matches the household staff's description and the Worths' testimony," Tim added, solemnly.

"Does Richmond have a local police station?"

"Still an unofficial constable," answered Tim. "They

do have an undertaker though."

"Younger, if you're fit, I need you to fetch whoever serves as constable, and the undertaker."

Younger nodded, and trotted towards the black bore, eager to leave the scene. As the young man disappeared from view, Riot turned to the remains of his client's wife.

Something niggled at the back of his mind. He removed his gloves and folded back the jacket, exposing a sliced shirtwaist, unhooked corset, torn chemise, and bruised skin. Riot probed the damp chemise, rubbing the material between his fingers. Not linen or silk, but a thin cotton blend. In contrast, the corset was silk, richly embroidered. The laces, however, ran up the sides and it was unlike any corset he had ever seen. He tilted his head in consideration. One of the stays was missing. With a shift of clothing, he revealed the edge, fished a magnifying glass from his pocket and flipped the round glass from its case.

"Find something?" Tim asked.

"A steel stay is missing. The fabric wasn't cut or torn, but rather, the thread was plucked along the hem."

"Maybe she was meaning to have it repaired?"

"Perhaps." Riot folded the torn clothing back in place, preserving the dead woman's modesty. He slid his finger along the fine black embroidery of the jacket. "This matching jacket and skirt must have cost a small fortune— the corset too. Everything except the chemise."

Tim scratched his beard. "What are you thinking?"

"That this case is rather complicated."

24

The Queen of Hearts

THURSDAY, JANUARY 4, 1900

A BLUR OF CARDS passed from one hand to the next. Rhythmic, constant, soothing. All fifty-two cards exchanged in a smooth flurry. Riot's sure hands mimicked his mind, shuffling facts, rearranging them, testing their validity and meaning. He sat slumped in his armchair, feet propped on Ravenwood's chair, surrounded by crates, dwelling in a state of uncertainty. One that his state of undress mirrored: stripped to his shirtsleeves, cuffs rolled up to his elbows, tie discarded, collar undone.

The narrow bed that Miss Lily had had her boys drag into the turret room remained undisturbed. Despite a long night, sleep had been elusive, and riddled with dreams and memory and ache. It had all started in this room.

As it had been three years ago, Riot hadn't wanted to find a body. And once again, he had failed. Too late; always too damn late.

Riot had accepted Alex Kingston's fury, Marcus Amsel's grief and his wife's stoic suffering, in silence. Throughout the meeting at the undertaker's, he had kept his cards close, gauging their reactions. Alex Kingston had not been bluffing. The man's fury was as real as the earth. And Riot was beginning to doubt his instincts.

A knock interrupted his thoughts. "Come."

A small head poked around the corner. Wide brown eyes looked into the room. A larger hand nudged the boy, and Tobias stumbled in, followed by his brother Grimm.

"We did as you asked, Mr. Riot," Tobias said. Grimm's eyes roved around the dark room, searching the shadows, passing the stack of newspapers strewn over the floor, before settling on the disheveled gentleman in the chair. The blur of cards shifting and shuffling in Riot's hands mesmerized the pair.

"Time?"

"Between fifteen and twenty minutes," Tobias replied. "We drove from Nob Hill to Market three different ways to be sure."

"Good work." Riot fished a half dollar out of his pocket and flipped it towards Tobias. The boy caught it easily. "For your troubles."

"No trouble at all, Mr. Riot," the boy said, setting a watch and its chain reverently on the table. "Did you find the lady?"

The cards stopped. Grimm tensed. And Tobias waited with hopeful eyes. However, Riot's silence was all the answer the pair received. They left him to his thoughts.

The cards changed their tune, the deck was cut, split,

divided. Riot applied pressure to their backs, brought them closer, and an arch of movement exploded in his hands. One card fell over the next, rearranging the deck. He closed his eyes, let his head fall back, and ran a finger along the perfect stack, probing the edges with a delicate touch.

The pieces did not fit. The unexpected departure, the drab coat, the mismatched undergarments. Given Mrs. Kingston's nature, she didn't seem the type to wait in a ferry terminal for nearly two hours. So what had she been doing? Was it as Kingston first suspected, an affair?

Riot hooked a finger around the deck, sliding the bottom card from the pile. He opened his eyes and held up the card. The King of Diamonds.

Footsteps echoed up the winding stairway, moving to the hallway outside. Tim stomped inside, grumbling and ill-mannered, with a tall man on his heels. Matthew Smith was large, broad-shouldered, and solid. His sandy hair was carefully parted and slicked. Despite the shadows circling his eyes and the pale stubble dusting his chin, he was neatly attired—a testament to his brief occupation as a patrolman.

"A damn waste of time," Tim grunted. Riot nodded to Smith. Tim had recruited the ex-patrolman last year. The young man had potential, but Riot had no inclination to train another detective. He wanted to wash his hands of the agency. Let it die with its founder. As such, he kept his feet firmly planted on Ravenwood's chair.

"I take it our ruffians didn't attempt to pick up their ransom payment for a dead hostage?"

"No," Tim said, planting his hide on the foot of the unused bed. "Poor Amsel stood on that dock all night."

"A hard thing for a man his age," Riot noted with a

pang. He liked Marcus Amsel. "A pity he listened to Kingston." There had been no convincing Kingston of the futility of his planned ambush. Vengeance, however, was like a burr in the heart.

"We kept an eye on Kingston, just like you asked, stayed a ways back from the dock, hid up on a ridge," Smith added, perching on a crate. "The gentleman was fuming all night. Thought he'd start firing his rifle for lack of anything better to do."

"This whole business is a mess," Tim remarked. "The police are tearing apart the fishing village near where she was found and questioning the railway workers."

"And Kingston's already placed a reward in the papers for information leading to the capture of his wife's murderers," Smith added.

"That will certainly muddy the waters," noted Riot, watching the hypnotic flutter of cards in his hands. "Any word on the *Magpie* from your boys?"

"Not yet. You want me to keep them searching? Kingston's convinced we're incompetent. We're off the case."

"Has that ever stopped us before?" Riot squared his deck with a tap, and studied the perfectly aligned edges.

"Can't say it has," Tim said with a chuckle. "What now, A.J.?"

Riot slipped a card from the center of the deck, twirled it once on his finger, and held it up to his eyes.

The Queen of Hearts.

"I, Mr. Von Poppin, intend to question our resident prostitute about her unmentionables." Smith and Tim blinked. Riot stood, slipped the Queen in his shirt pocket, plucked up his waistcoat and walked downstairs, leaving two puzzled men in his wake.

25

An Unmentionable Clue

RIOT STOOD BEFORE RAVENWOOD'S old consultation room. He worked the last cufflink through its hole, and politely tapped his knuckle against wood. Keen hearing picked up the swish of fabric, a breath of steps that graced the floor, followed by an inquiring call. The hour wasn't obscene, but it was early for anyone who led a nocturnal life.

"Atticus Riot," he answered through the door. "Sorry to disturb you, ma'am, but I hoped I might have a moment of your time."

Miss Lily's daughter, Maddie, appeared around the corner as the door opened. The girl glanced at the pair, eyes sliding from the silk-robed woman to the gentleman at her door. Maddie appeared more bemused than offended, hurrying past without comment.

"You're all the talk of the house, Mr. Riot," the woman said. Her voice was as sultry as her body, a tall, shapely woman with a mass of auburn hair that begged to be undone. "Hardly how I envisioned our introduction."

"Nor I," he replied smoothly.

"I'm sure you've heard a few things about me."

"I have," he admitted, "but not your name."

"Annie Dupree."

"A pleasure, Miss Dupree." He brushed his lips over her offered hand.

"Won't you come in, Mr. Riot?" She stepped back, opening the door in invitation. Riot accepted, stepping into her boudoir with trepidation. Not because of the lady's presence, but because of the memories he feared were waiting.

Miss Dupree's eyes roved over her guest, admiring his poise and the cut of his trousers. "Sit, if you wish. May I offer you a drink, Mr. Riot?" She sauntered towards a velvet settee and chair, robe brushing against her calves.

"No, thank you," he said, relaxing. Alert tension bled onto the plush carpet. There were no lurking shadows. "The room has changed, for the better I might add." Transformed, more like, from a den of masculinity to a feminine heaven. A large, draped bed dominated the room, while an ornamental screen created a nook that served as a sitting area.

"I'm glad you approve," she smiled, and took a seat, crossing her legs. Silk slid over silk, exposing a pale leg and a soft shoulder. "I imagined it would only be a matter of time before you called on me. I've never been secretive about my preferred profession, but I assure you that I *am* discreet."

Riot sat in the chair opposite, leaning forward and

interlacing his fingers. "I haven't come to discuss your profession, Miss Dupree."

A slight catch of her breath hinted at her concern, while a flutter of dark lash confirmed her worry. "I'm partial to these rooms, Mr. Riot. I'm sure we can come to some sort of arrangement—"

"Miss Dupree," Riot interrupted, holding up a steady hand. "I require your assistance."

"Most men do," she purred.

"Not of that sort." Riot smoothed his beard, and tilted his head in amusement as the awkwardness of the situation settled in the room. "I need your expertise on a woman's unmentionables."

The edge of her full lip curved. "And here I thought I'd heard every possible request that could leave a man's tongue. I do believe this is a first, Mr. Riot."

"I strive to excite, Miss Dupree."

Her eyes flashed. "Of that I'm sure," she replied. "I can't imagine why you would need my expertise. You strike me as a man who is more than familiar with a woman's underpinnings."

"A gentleman never tells."

"Nor should they ask."

"An exception, in this case. I hope your insights will help me bring a woman's murderer to justice."

Her flirtatious facade faded, but only for a moment before she reached for familiarity. "My talents are at your disposal."

Riot described Mrs. Kingston's attire in detail. When he fell silent, Miss Dupree exchanged seduction for perplexity like a mask. She smoothed the silk robe over her knee, staring at the flowered print with a thoughtful pout of red lips.

"You're describing an athletic corset, Mr. Riot. Not many women choose to wear such an undergarment when they intend to be seduced, which is why, I imagine, you've never seen its like."

"I'll give you that, Miss Dupree." Riot tipped his chin in acknowledgement. "What do you find puzzling about this lady's ensemble?"

"You can buy such corsets ready-made; however, from what you've described—the side-lacing, the silk and small embellishments—it's a tailored garment. As is the dress. I can't imagine a woman wearing such a stylish dress with that type of corset. And then, of course, you have the chemise."

"It seemed unusually plain."

"Certainly to a man like you." Miss Dupree leaned back, draped an arm over the back of the settee, and toyed with a tendril of escaped hair. "I'm not surprised the material struck you. Probably batiste. Very cheap, very thin, and as you say, plain."

"And not a material suited to exertion."

"Silk or a fine linen would be my choice."

"What of the missing stay?"

"A misplaced stay can be lethal," she answered. "If the material were to rip or tear, and a stay emerged, it would need to be removed immediately or it might puncture the skin."

"And what would a woman do if her corset were attempting such a murder?"

"She would mend it immediately, or send it off to be mended. Most women have more than one corset, but if the woman were exceptionally poor, she might remove the stay; however, the fit would hardly be comfortable."

Riot frowned. Why would a wealthy woman wear a

stylish dress with a drab coat, and wear a flimsy chemise with a well-made athletic corset that was missing a stay rendering it uncomfortable?

"It sounds as though you have a puzzle on your hands."

"Yes," he murmured. "With pieces that do not fit."

"Never an issue in my line of work," Miss Dupree breathed, glancing at her nails. A sudden thought struck Riot, and his breath caught.

"Thank you, Miss Dupree," he said, standing abruptly. "Your expertise has been invaluable."

"I aim to satisfy every man who enters my boudoir."

Riot paused, mid-bow, and glanced at her. The edge of his lip twitched. "Enjoy the rest of your morning, ma'am."

26

A Lingering Question

A SYMPHONY OF SNORES rumbled from the turret room. Atticus Riot pushed the door open and was greeted by two exhausted detectives. Tim had commandeered the narrow bed, leaving Smith to fend for himself. The large man was sprawled on a pile of drapery.

Although the room was in a perpetual state of transition, with an occupant who wasn't sure whether he was coming or going, Miss Lily had seen to his basic necessities. A wash basin, pitcher, and mirror had been provided. And despite his protestations, she had unpacked his Gladstone along with the recently delivered trunk from the ferry. His shirts were ironed, his coats brushed, and his hats hung on their hooks.

Riot didn't know where Tim had found the woman, but as always, the man was an excellent judge of character.

The small round mirror told Riot that he was in need of a trim. He grimaced at his ruffled reflection. Hardly a suitable state to have called on Miss Dupree.

'*You've only just realized?*' came a remonstrating voice. Riot glanced at Ravenwood's empty chair, scowled, and reached for his revolver. Flesh gripped ivory, and a nickel barrel slid from its nest of leather.

Tim snorted and jerked awake. "Trouble?" he asked groggily. Smith blinked himself upright, looking abashed.

"A precaution." Riot pulled the revolver's latch, bent back stock and barrel, and checked the chambers. Satisfied, he clicked the break top shut and slid his No. 3 into its holster, then transferred the harness from its hook onto his shoulders. A hard, comforting weight pressed against his ribs. "I think it too convenient that Kingston's warehouse was sabotaged and his landau had a damaged spring on the same day his wife was abducted."

"I don't follow, Mr. Riot," Smith admitted. "The lady was seen on the ferry."

"The two missing hours, Mr. Smith," Riot announced, choosing a homburg for his excursion. He settled the stiff felt on top of his head with reverence. As always, it fit perfectly. "What was Mrs. Kingston doing before she boarded the 9:00 ferry?"

"Waiting at the ferry station," Smith said, slowly, more question than fact.

"Doubtful," Riot corrected.

"How so?"

"The drab coat, gentlemen."

"It'd help if you shared your thoughts," muttered Tim.

"Not before they're confirmed."

"Just you wait, Smith. After it's all said and done, A.J. here will claim he knew what happened all along."

"One must have the pieces before the puzzle can be assembled," Riot drawled.

Tim ignored this simple bit of logic. "How did you find Miss Dupree's undergarments?"

"Quite informative."

"I'm sure they were." Tim clucked his tongue. "Where you off to now?"

"First, to a barber," Riot said, shrugging on his coat, "and then I'll be combing the dance halls for a pretty young man."

27

The Second Son

THE OFFICES OF CURTIS Amsel dwelt in the shadows of two opposing buildings, the *Call* and the *Chronicle* on Market. The *Call's* baroque dome rose imperiously over the *Chronicle's* practical clock tower—two stony rivals, eyeing one another across a bustling street.

The waiting room had all the touches of a prosperous firm, or at the very least one wanting to give that impression. A young clerk sat behind the divider, at a curved desk, alternating between typewriter and telephone. Every time the telephone rang, Riot resisted the urge to reach for his revolver. Telephones, in his opinion, were a damn nuisance.

A door behind the divider opened, spewing out one gentleman and inviting the next inside. The typewriter ceased its banging.

"Mr. Amsel will see you now, Mr. Riot," the clerk said.

A tall, thin man stretched out a hand to Riot. He was a younger version of his father, possessing the same cheerful blue eyes and easy amiability. Sandy hair, tailored suit, and bow-tie were all in perfect order.

"Mr. Riot," Curtis Amsel greeted. "I apologize for the delay."

"No need. I wasn't expected." Riot eyed the man's roll top desk, orderly pigeon holes, and a wall of deep shelves that contained long rolls of schematics. A neat drafting table occupied one wall and a row of windows offered a view of baroque detailing.

At Mr. Amsel's offer, Riot sat, studying the engineer as he took his accustomed place. There was a tightness at the corner of Curtis' eyes and lips. A crease of strain on an otherwise cheery disposition.

"Work, I find, is the only remedy for grief," Curtis explained, shuffling papers from one side of his desk to the other. "You have my gratitude, Mr. Riot. At the very least, there is a body to bury. Have you found the men responsible?"

"I hoped you might be able to assist."

Curtis glanced up, surprise erasing exhaustion. "I am at your service."

"Some answers would be appreciated."

"Of course." Curtis faced Riot square, folding his hands on the desk.

"Did your sister ever visit you in the city?"

"I saw Isobel now and again, around town, mostly at social functions. She came here often, whether or not I was in my office." Curtis gestured to a shelf of books. "She loved to read—even these." Riot scanned the heavy tomes: engineering, mathematics, and law. "But then Isobel always had unconventional tastes."

Riot smiled. "It appears you shared those unconventional tastes."

"I'm an engineer, Mr. Riot. These books are my livelihood."

"Why do you think your sister was interested in them?"

Curtis shrugged, eyebrows and hands moving upwards with a comical effect. "Who is to say. Reason and Isobel are not two words our family ever used in the same sentence."

"Were you close to your sister?"

"With twenty-three years separating us, I was more father than brother. Throughout her short but eventful life, it seemed I was always bailing her out of trouble." Curtis sighed heavily. "In this one instance, I failed."

"Your father mentioned that you hushed the press on at least two occasions. How were you able to accomplish that?"

Color rose in an unforgiving complexion. "I have a number of satisfied clients in high places, Mr. Riot. I exchanged work, at considerable cost to my firm, for a measure of silence."

"I imagine scandal would have hurt your own business interests," Riot observed. "A young woman's indiscretions reflect on an entire family."

"In certain circles, yes," Curtis agreed. "My interventions were far from altruistic."

"It appears your sister did well for herself over the summer."

"So it seemed," Curtis said, reluctantly. "I was apprehensive about introducing her to society, but she seemed to have learn a degree of civility. Or at the very least, Mother put the fear of God in her after she nearly caused a scandal by running off without a chaperone in Europe. Even after she settled into polite society, I was always expectant. Isobel is—was—prone to hysterics."

"That's a fairly broad term," Riot noted. "How so?"

"Extreme mood shifts. Bursts of energy and wild ideas followed by foul moods and long stretches of solitude. And the stories—" Curtis' voice caught. He blinked rapidly, and when he found his voice, it was raw with grief. "I do believe I will miss her stories."

"Any in particular?"

"Name your fairytale: dime novels, time travel, conspiracies, ghosts." Curtis rubbed his temple, the perfect picture of a long-suffering parent.

"Yet she had an interest in mathematics and law." Riot gestured towards the shelves.

"Isobel was mercurial. As unpredictable as the sea. One never knew in which direction the wind would blow. Quite honestly, I was surprised to find her alive at the end of the day." Curtis grimaced at his own words, regretting them instantly. "An ill comment under the circumstances. Forgive me. May I ask how my mother and father are doing?"

"As to be expected."

"I telephoned them, but one can only say so much over the line. As soon as I finish this contract—" He waved a vague hand towards the drafting table.

"I wonder if you might be able to shed some light on a point that has been troubling me."

"I'll try."

"Your sister enrolled at university, but only weeks later announced her engagement to Alex Kingston. Was she in love with Kingston?"

Curtis began to laugh, low and bitter. "Good Lord, but

that's a perfect example to illustrate my point. Over the summer, Isobel came to me, claiming that Alex Kingston was orchestrating Father's ruin. She had no proof of course. Her claims were so outlandish that I told her to leave a man like Kingston alone. And the next thing I know, she's marrying him."

"Was she happy?"

"It seemed so."

"What was her theory?"

"That he was arranging accidents to benefit his clients. Everything from arson, to murder, to punching holes in bags of flour. Utterly absurd. Alex Kingston is simply good at his job."

Riot studied Curtis over an expanse of wood, letting the man's own words sink into the ensuing quiet. Curtis resumed shifting papers on his desk. The lines returned, etched into his fair features.

"You weren't concerned that she married a man whom she accused of grave crimes?"

"If she had been any other woman—" Curtis shook his head. "No, not Isobel. Do you know, Mr. Riot, she was the flower girl at my wedding. Six years old. Half way down the aisle, she stopped, pulled out a cigarette, lit it, and smoked it up to the altar."

Riot cleared his throat, suppressing a laugh. "I assume she didn't approve of your marriage."

"Isobel was spoiled," Curtis stated, bluntly. "Utterly mad as a hatter. Father should have sent her to a lady's school long before she reached fifteen, or better yet, to a convent."

"You have been enlightening, Mr. Amsel." Riot stood and made to leave, but at the door, he turned. "You wouldn't happen to know where your brother Lotario is living?"

Curtis pressed his lips together. At length, he answered, "Not precisely, but I do know he lives in the city. He works in the theatre, or so Father tells anyone who asks. However, I do not count burlesque and bawdy shows as employment. If that's all, Mr. Riot, I have work to finish before I can visit my grieving parents."

28

The Narcissist

ATTICUS RIOT THREADED HIS way through squalor and wealth, one interwoven with the other, creating a grotesque and wondrous tapestry of life.

Sunlight rarely touched the cobblestones. Brick and wood blotted out the sky, reducing the vast unknown to a distant slice. Banners crisscrossed the crack in the city like cobwebs clamoring for silent attention. The signs were loud and persistent, like hawkers for the eyes. Rotting vegetables, spices, tobacco, and incense filled the teeming maze. A throng of silk and long queues, of flat hats and bowlers, milled through the narrow lane along with a pungent sweetness and a tide of ebbing tongues.

Here, all manner of markets flourished, selling fish, fruit, and flesh.

Pigs hung from hooks, turtles languished in boxes,

twisted, unknown roots sat side by side with familiar fruit. Clothing merchants battled with grocers for space, and opium dens clashed with havens of silk. Rows of shacks lined the street, narrow doors with a patch of bars, where pearl white faces stared forlornly through the gaps, calling to strange men. Dangerous men, in loose blouses and wide silk belts stood guard, keeping order over the cribs and the lines of men eager to sate their lust.

Nothing had changed. Ownership swapped hands, the Kings and Queens of the Barbary Coast towered and toppled, but the trade remained. Murderers and cutthroats for hire, sailors drunk on rum, runners and crimpers, whores and scoundrels.

Ravenwood and Riot had spent nearly twenty years chasing criminals through the alleyways of the Barbary Coast. Slavers, thieves, drug lords, and pimps. When one lord of the underworld fell, another rose to take his place, or simply continued his enterprise from a cozy cell that was bought with graft and fortune.

Opium and slavery were lucrative businesses, protected by the very men who lived in luxury, lording over an empire of lives from high hills that were impossible to see from the depths of depravity.

A hopeless girl locked eyes with Riot through her cage. Her dark eyes mirrored his own. In a monotonous, sing-song voice, she called out her price in broken English. A freckled boy with a mop of red hair and not more than twelve years old, paid his fifteen cents and was ushered through the narrow door.

As long as money flowed, the dregs of society would follow. There was no damming the currents. At Riot's urging, Ravenwood had tried. And died.

'*And so did you.*'

Riot pushed the thought aside. Ravenwood's sacrifice had simply diverted the river. Corruption in San Francisco was as rampant as ever.

A wide square with sparse trees opened to a sky that was dreary and silver in the afternoon mist. Rows of brick and mortar hugged the square, facing each other across the expanse of green. *The Bella Union*, the once-famed concert hall, was now a penny arcade and wax museum.

The edge of Riot's lip quirked. Perhaps some things did change after all.

Kearny was bustling with delivery wagons and hacks. However, compared to the night, the street was quiet. Grocers and clothing shops opened their doors, squashed between dance halls and brothels advertising pretty waiter girls and bawdy entertainments.

The street was a sad state in daylight. Electric signs and red lights resisted the brightness of life, stripped of their luster in the colorless day. But in darkness and mist, they pulsed with vibrancy. The streets thrived in a cloak of obscurity, and men took comfort in anonymity. At night they were a motley bunch, a throng of shadowed faces and hungry eyes, milling about brothels and dance halls like rats roaming a sewer.

A mob of boys rushed Riot, eager to hand out paste-board cards for harlots and fliers for dance halls. He waved off their advertisements, and navigated the street, timing his crossing between a milk wagon and a hack full of wide-eyed socialites gawking at the Barbary Coast.

The morning had been an uneventful one, and the afternoon was proving tedious. It felt as though he had crossed Kearny's cobblestones a hundred times since leaving the barber, searching concert halls and dives, asking after a young man by the name of Lotario. Turning east, he made a sharp right down a narrow side street. The sky disappeared, crowded out by laundry lines and rickety staircases that led to dark holes.

A circular sign, trimmed in gold, was thrust into the alley on an iron rod: *The Narcissist.* Unlike the other ostentatious signs and dead lights that proclaimed ladies aplenty, this front door was subdued. A dark portal with a single red-paned lantern hung in a recessed archway.

Riot tapped his stick on the door. A slat slid to the side. Eyes roved over his attire. "I'm here to see Paris," he said.

"Isn't everyone?" replied a cheerful voice. The portal opened. Riot exchanged grey bricks and refuse for a marble entry hall. A giant mural, in which a group of muscular young men competed in ancient games, demanded the eye. It was obvious, from the naked display of masculinity, that they quite enjoyed their sport.

The chiseled doorman, whose chest was testing the limits of shirt and waistcoat, accepted Riot's hat, stick, and gloves. After opening his coat, and subsequently surrendering his revolver, Riot was shown into a parlor, where more pretty young men frolicked on the walls. Music and conversation drifted lightly through the room, hinting at other guests and an air of secrecy. Twin David statues, whose proportions had been considerably embellished, stood guard beside a heavy velvet curtain.

At the swish of satin, Riot turned. A woman draped in green and blue smiled in greeting. Her pronounced Adam's apple and square jaw hinted at another gender.

"Welcome to the *Narcissist*, sir," her deep voice contradicted the lip rouge and luscious locks of hair. "There's no need for names. All our guests remain anonymous. You may call me Hera, and I assure you, we can fulfill your every desire."

"I'm told you have a dancer here by the name of Paris." Through painstaking leg work, perusing many a Madam's collection, and countless false leads, Riot had finally discerned Lotario's stage name. "A young, tanned man with golden hair."

"Paris isn't taking any visitors today, but we have many others, just as beautiful."

"It's a personal matter."

"Are you a friend?"

"Atticus Riot." He produced his card. At the sight of the pasteboard, Hera's lips tightened. "The matter doesn't concern your establishment, nor is your prize dancer in any sort of trouble." His words smoothed her ruffled feathers.

In short order, and little fuss, Riot was escorted past the twin Davids, through a curtain, and up a staircase by a sleek, black-suited man in tails. As the hallway progressed, the frolicking young men became less restricted in their activities.

The escort stopped in front of a door, and knocked primly. "*Monsieur* Paris," he called in a high voice. "*Monsieur* Riot to see you."

"I'm in no mood, Dominic," a light, drawling voice pushed under the door.

"It's about your sister," Riot said simply. The key turned in the lock, and the door opened.

The room was dark, lit by a single gas lamp. Riot let his eyes adjust to the dimness. A slim figure stood in the center of the room, wearing loose trousers and nothing else. The man was a contradiction of masculinity and feminine beauty: lush, golden hair, lithe and athletic, slight and powerful. Yet, his eyes were bored, and dull with drink.

"Do you prefer Paris or Lotario?"

Lotario did not answer. He turned, swaying towards a divan. He reached for a brandy snifter and lounged against the cushions, eyes roving lazily over his guest.

A newspaper laid on the floor, discarded, a single spot of reality amid the silk and velvet opulence. "I had to read about my twin's death in the newspapers," Lotario remarked, noting Riot's gaze.

"You're not an easy man to find."

"I'm surprised my family spoke of me at all."

"You were in a photograph." Riot nudged a mound of cushions off a nearby chair, and sat, studying the young man. Time, vermin, and gulls had disfigured the corpse he had found on the beach, but what had been left of the woman was certainly similar to the face in front of him.

"You're the fellow who found my twin's body." Lotario nodded towards the paper at his feet. Riot did not answer. Paling, the young man gulped down his brandy, teeth clicking against glass. "Little good that did anyone, especially Isobel. Why does it matter that you found me?" Lacquered nails tapped impatiently on the snifter.

"Doesn't justice count for something?"

"Finding her murderers won't bring her back." Lotario stood abruptly, an explosion of coiled muscle and graceful urgency, swaying towards the sideboard. Riot understood the lad's anger perfectly. He had been in his shoes—still was. But no matter how hard one fought, the cards never changed, only their order.

"How *did* you find me?"

"Your father mentioned your name," Riot answered. "He said you were an entertainer in San Francisco."

"That certainly narrows things down," Lotario drawled with a smirk. "So you naturally assumed I was entertaining men with 'unnatural desires'?"

"Your father also mentioned that you studied abroad, and that you and Isobel were close. When he told me of her adventures on the continent, I thought it strange that she was found in Venice with an artist *and* a fencer under one roof. Friends of yours?"

"Father thought Isobel was being quite naughty." Lotario chuckled. "Unfortunately, telling mother and father the truth would have been little better."

"Weren't you concerned about your sister's reputation?"

"Their assumptions amused Isobel. And it kept them from asking more questions."

"Was she protecting you?"

"Sentiment is lost on Isobel." Lotario smiled like a cat with its paw in the cream. "But it's irrelevant now. Why exactly have you come, Mr. Riot?"

"I'm looking for answers."

"I can't help you there."

"On the morning your sister was abducted, Alex Kingston left his home at 6:45." Lotario wrinkled his nose. "Your sister told the staff that she was going to spend Christmas in Sausalito, and left shortly after her husband, at approximately 7:00. A journey from Nob Hill to the foot of Market takes fifteen to twenty minutes. And although there was a 7:30 ferry, she was seen on the 9:00. I would like to know where your sister went."

"Window shopping?"

"Your sister doesn't strike me as the frivolous sort."

"She wasn't. And yes, she came to visit me as you obviously suspect. It's only a short walk from California—for someone as fit as Isobel at any rate."

"Why didn't you contact someone when news of her

abduction reached the papers?"

"What was there to say?" Lotario sat forward, brushing his hair from his face. In the light of the brandy and reflection of glass, his eyes shone amber, and his hair, gold. "Isobel and I visited when we could—that was until Kingston married her. I hadn't seen her in months."

"You dislike Kingston?"

"I haven't met him, but I could tell she was unhappy."

"Why do you think she married Kingston?"

"I don't know, Mr. Riot. Isobel was always an enigma, even to me—her twin. She was as cold-blooded as a shark. I always thought we were given the wrong bodies. She would have made an excellent man, and I, a woman. What I wouldn't give to shed my skin for hers."

"Cold-blooded?"

"Bel never did anything without reason. She treated life like a game of chess. While I yearned for approval, she never cared what others thought of her—of her reputation, of repercussions, of tarnishing the family name. Such considerations were beneath her notice, and yet mother and father doted on her while I was cast from the family."

"What did you talk about when she visited?"

"She was in a hurry, as always." He shrugged, a slight lift of one slim shoulder. "She asked me to come to Sausalito with her and repair my relationship with the family. As if *I* were the one who had caused the rift. The suggestion was absurd, but she had one of those whims in her head, like she had when we were young. By God, the places I followed her, trying to keep her out of trouble. I still have nightmares about the old mine shafts near our home." Lotario closed his eyes, rubbing his temple with the side of his snifter.

"What was her whim in this particular case?"

"She wanted to sail the bay again. I told her to take the yacht herself. She knows I don't care for that sort of thing anymore."

"The yacht?"

"*My* yacht," he clarified. "Father and I built it together. I took it when I left. It's rotting alongside a fisherman's dock." Lotario chuckled at some inner musing.

"What is it called?"

"I renamed it the *Pagan Lady* just to spite father. I doubt he even knows, but it pleased me at the time."

"Where is the boat docked?"

"The Green Street Wharf." Lotario waved a languid hand.

"Was your sister planning on sailing to Sausalito?"

"The boat is in need of maintenance, Mr. Riot. Hardly seaworthy. I told her as much but that didn't deter her enthusiasm. She said we could take one of father's boats once we arrived in Sausalito. I told her I'd never go back home, that I wasn't welcome." Lotario finished off his brandy with a long swallow. "She seemed to accept that, but intended to go sailing anyway—alone. She asked for suitable clothing. Apparently Kingston didn't much care for his wife owning trousers."

"You gave her a set of gentleman's clothes?"

"Of a rough sort. We're the same size." He gestured around the silk laden room. "Nothing that I'd wear now."

"Did your sister say anything else?"

Lotario frowned into his empty glass. When he spoke, his voice was hoarse. "She asked if I had any envelopes and postage marks. Then she asked me not to hate her and said goodbye. I should have gone with her."

Riot cleared his throat. "Where do you keep your

envelopes?"

Lotario looked puzzled, annoyed that the stranger in his room should ask such an insignificant question after so dramatic a statement.

"In my writing desk."

"May I see?"

Lotario huffed, gesturing towards the elegant desk. Riot rose, and turned the key in its lock, rolling the top back. A perfectly orderly sight greeted him.

"Isobel was disgusted with its state," Lotario said, moving to his side. "She insisted on restoring order—all in her quest for an envelope."

"Where, may I ask," Riot began slowly, as he opened each drawer. "do you keep your proof of ownership for your craft?"

"It's in there somewhere."

With Lotario's permission, Riot spent the next half hour rifling through papers. However, the proof of ownership for the *Pagan Lady* was not present.

29

The Empty Berth

THE DOCKMASTER STOMPED HIS way down the pier. He was red-faced and puffing, irritable as a roused coon. And as fragrant.

"She was right there, in that there berth, there." The dockmaster threw a meaty hand at the dingy water, strewn with flotsam and refuse. "Like I said, I spotted a young man on board the *Pagan Lady* on Tuesday morning. I keep an eye on my dock, I do. A slight fellow, blond hair sticking out from beneath his cap. A bit of a Nancy boy if you ask me, but he had proof of ownership. Told me he was planning on taking her out to sea, and wondered if I'd outfit her for a price. And I says, 'Sure. As fine a vessel as she is, not being taken out to sea more often than not, it ain't right.'"

Riot considered the empty space. And then the maze

of bristling masts, huddled around the docks. Thousands of vessels, from cutters, to sloops, to launches, ferries, arks, and great four-masted steam ships.

"A fine gaff-rigged cutter, she is," the dockmaster declared. "I didn't mind outfitting her at all. So I done like he paid me to do. Generous he was."

"When did he return?"

"The young gentleman, Lotario was his name, returned early on Friday. He seemed in a bad way. Lingered onboard his craft, he did; kept to his cabin."

"How was he in a bad way?"

"Limping, had a pretty blinker, moved real stiff like. This time he was wearing a Chinaman's clothes." The dockmaster chuckled. "The lad likely paid his dime at a creep joint, and got his billfold pinched for a lick of his prick, then beat for the hell of it. Stay out of the Barbary Coast, I say. Not the first young man rarin' to explore its fleshly delights, only to find trouble."

Riot frowned in thought, adjusting his spectacles. He squinted past the setting sun towards Lotario's apartments, buried in a sea of brick and mortar. A wall of fog was rolling through the Gate, drowning the falling sun. Light and mist warred, setting the sky on fire.

"When did she sail?"

"On Saturday. I was a bit worried about the lad, smarting as he was, single-handling her, but once I helped him raise the sail, he proved himself able and the wind favorable."

"A pity," Riot murmured. "I had hoped to make an offer to buy her."

The dockmaster eyed the gentleman skeptically. He proved a perceptive fellow, for Riot was clearly a dirt dweller. "Well," the dockmaster huffed, combing his mustache with his fingers, "the lad didn't take her far. Friend o' mine saw the Lady just today."

"Where?"

"Just a few wharves down," the dockmaster pointed north. "In the jam at Fisherman's Wharf."

30

A Shark in Water

WEDNESDAY, DECEMBER 27, 1899
EIGHT DAYS EARLIER

THE BLOOD FROZE IN her body. Ice clenched her limbs. The first shock of cold was familiar. Pain was replaced with heart-skipping ache. Her skull throbbed. One all-consuming constriction, and then a burst. Instinct screamed for relief. Hands twitched, flailing in blackness. Isobel embraced the panic like an old friend, calming her thoughts.

The boat. Gunshots. If she emerged, they would either capture her anew, or shoot. She preferred the latter. Harnessing her body's desire to escape a watery death, she pulled herself through the water, sensing currents, feeling their pull, orienting herself with the tides like a natural predator.

Her body was numb; the pain in her bones was stifled, but her limbs were clumsy, and something tore up her side with every stroke.

The breath in her lungs turned toxic. Slowly, she exhaled until her lungs were hollow, a void between her ribs. Her body began to sink. With calm determination, as if she had all the time in the world, she began to climb.

The world compressed, and then popped. Cold air slapped her face. She responded like a newborn babe gulping in its first breath. Curses filled the night, bouncing off the sea. A monstrous shadow floated beneath the moon. A glow of distant lights illuminated the shadow's shape. A trawler. Single mast. Shapes moved from stern to aft.

"Ya daft bastard, Cox!" a lilting voice slammed into the water, bouncing off in all directions. "Why'd you go and shoot our payload?"

Isobel was being dragged farther away from the boat into emptiness and a vast abyss. She tried to think as she slipped off her rotted boots. Then she treaded water, willing a sluggish, hard-bitten brain into action.

"The bitch took my eye!" the man called Cox roared.

"She put a hole in my side, and I didn't do the same," the slim Irishman snapped. "Shut your trap now. You might 'ave missed."

The ox fell silent. They were listening for her splashes, her struggles, even a cry for help. Isobel remained quiet, gently treading water, resisting the urge to swim away and betray her position.

One light pulsed in the distance, to the far right of the greater glow. She turned her neck, chin brushing saltwater, and saw another light, a closer one, pulsing in the abyss.

Two lighthouses and a large glow directly behind the trawler currently drifting on its moorings. She closed her eyes, listening, navigating the night and fog with bells and mournful horns, letting the current rescue her from human threat.

The stern swirled, turning murky in the dark, and the men's curses faded. She began to move, laboriously. Her breath came shallow and fast, as if she were still wearing a corset.

Slowly, she pulled herself towards the glow. Away from the lighthouse throbbing like a sluggish pulse on Goat Island. All the while, the currents dragged her towards the distant second—Alcatraz. She swam at an angle, knowing a maze of hulls and pilings waited. A safe haven. If she could only reach it, swimming without noise at a tedious crawl, flirting with danger, between drowning and recapture.

Isobel moved through the water, climbing swells, only to plummet into the valleys between, drifting farther and farther from shore. When the boat was lost to the night, she gritted her teeth and swam.

31

Eternity

THE NIGHT WAS ENDLESS. Motes of light rose and fell, never nearing, never quite disappearing. She was a moth caught in the breeze, striving towards a guiding light that taunted and teased.

It was eternity. Clawing through a remorseless sea.

If she stopped, gave into the cold—the ache and terror —her life would simply fade. She'd never be the wiser. Surrender to the tug and current. One breath, one blissful release, and she'd drift in peace. There were those who would mourn, and those who would rejoice. However, the Ivory King would reign victorious.

Determination rose with a swell, and a second wind beat at her sails. Reluctant to retire, Isobel fought, sliding through murk towards a faraway glow. The current lost its hold, lights neared, shapes rose from the sea, and the water calmed. Her hand slapped wood.

32

The Fisherman's Catch

THE CREAK OF WOOD and rope surrounded her. Voices
drifted in the fog. Shadows loomed, distorted in the eerie
glow. Like a rat swimming through a wreckage, Isobel
slipped through the maze, circling boats, some dark and
others guarded, lanterns swaying like will o' the wisps,
seducing her with warmth and promise.

Surf slapped against a barrier. A shifting of sludge
around the wharves. Stench filled her nostrils: fish guts,
refuse, and human waste swirled in an aimless whirlpool.
Hulls scraped in greeting and crushing threat. She avoided
the gaps.

She felt her way along a slippery, squarish hull, bracing
against the wood lest the water shift, sending the boat
slamming into her face. The boat sat low in the water, its
rail within reach. Isobel kicked, slapped the top, but her

numb fingers slipped. She splashed back, disappearing beneath the water. When she emerged, a leathery face and slanted gaze stared over the rail with lantern held high.

"*Ai ya!*" The lantern in the man's hand came closer. Shock registered in his eyes. Quick voices and quicker feet. Panicking, Isobel pulled herself along the hull, seeking escape. A strong hand reached over the rail, snatching her braid. Like a fish, she was dragged over the side and flopped on deck, coughing and shivering with pain.

Three puzzled faces stared down at their catch. The lantern neared, blinding her, and illuminating the clinging chemise and bloomers. She nearly wept for its warmth.

Sing-song voices danced rapidly from one face to the next. Familiar words ending in long *Aaah's*. She rose on hands and knees, shaking from crown to heel. One of the faces disappeared, returning with warmth. Wool embraced, and she clung to the blanket. A bent, leathery-faced man helped her rise.

"Thank you," she chattered. And then her mind churned out the few words Hop had taught her as a child. "*Dò jeh.*"

The younger of the two men responded with a long string of words.

One word in the deluge leapt out at her. "No, please, no police." She shook her head, even as an old woman was leading her beneath the junk's canopy. Nets, ropes, traps, and clothing swayed from the cabin's ceiling. The old woman pointed to a straw mat on the floor, and Isobel sat, huddling in her blanket.

Musical words flowed over her, bouncing between the men in rising tempo. The old woman chopped her hand through the air, cutting through the men's argument. The men fell silent.

"Clothes," Isobel said, pointing to the coveted items hanging overhead. "I just need clothes."

The woman huffed in reply, and turned to the small cooking stove. Tea was poured, hot and steaming. A warm cup was pressed into Isobel's trembling hands. The woman said a soothing word. Her eyes were kind. As Isobel sat and drank, the younger man gathered clothing, folding the items with care before setting the pile by her mat with a deep bow.

All along, the older man sat, gazing at his catch with obvious pride. It wasn't every day a fisherman caught a young woman in his net.

33

Ponder and Plot

IN THE GREY DRIZZLE of early morning light, Isobel disembarked in the muck of Mission Bay. Her belly was full and her veins flowed with warm tea. She limped along the wharves, head lowered, braid tucked beneath a wide brimmed hat.

The wharves were swarming with activity, like a horde of industrious ants. She wove her way through dockworkers laden with timbers, tottering delivery wagons, and bartering merchants. Dressed in the loose blouse and straw hat of a shrimper, no one paid the limping Chinaman any heed.

What her rescuers, Keung Lung and his family, thought of the woman they'd fished from the sea, she did not know. It was best to not ask questions. Isobel had been thankful for their wisdom and polite distance, but most of all, for their help. They had offered her a safe haven. And after a day and a night in their care, she was much restored —if badly bruised.

The caged clock tower of the ferry building loomed in the fog. Its clock kept time, and its hands were nearly in the same position as when she'd last glimpsed it—so long ago, a lifetime, or so it seemed.

Isobel shut out the rumbling cable cars, bells, and rush of people clamoring at the gateway that led to all ends of the earth. She was tempted to board a ferry and flee.

"Bombardment of Ladysmith! Nine Boers killed, wagons lost!" a newsboy shouted the headlines in a shrill, hoarse voice. "Plague scare at the Hawaiian Isles! We could be next. Read it while it's hot!"

She focused on the waving newspaper in his hand: Friday December 29, 1899. The date anchored her firmly in the present.

Her reasons for lingering with the Lungs had been twofold: recuperation and thought. She'd had time to think, to ponder and plot. While fleeing was *one* option, it went against her nature.

First, she would buy a newspaper and rough clothes with the money she had stowed in her twin's boat. And then she would go a-hunting for three men and a trawler.

34

Three Bullets

THREE ENVELOPES SLIPPED THROUGH the post box slot.
Unseen, they tumbled on top of the stack. All three letters
carried identical messages. And unknowingly, all three
were as deadly as a bullet. Their sender walked on, disappearing in the throng of businessmen.

Isobel pulled her cap lower over her bruised face. She
slouched, hands in her peacoat, boots scuffing the planks.
She walked away from the post office on Battery, heading
towards Kearney, wondering where she should start.

Nob Hill climbed over the buildings, dominating her
thoughts. Doubt scratched at her mind like a burr. What if
her theories were incorrect? Would the Ivory King have
gone to these lengths to rid himself of a foe? Her opponent's side of the board was obscured. She could only
theorize. The urge to contact her family was

overwhelming; however, any insights gained would not be worth the price.

Isobel tore her eyes from the hill and her previous life. Her abductors had lost their captive, and their payload had vanished beneath the sea. Her thoughts mulled over the pieces, and her feet continued to move.

The men had wanted her alive. Obviously, for purposes of ransom. These had not been the usual men paid to keep an eye on her. But, of course, they wouldn't be. The watchers had been absent, on that one day after Christmas. All her precautions had been needless. The Ivory King had foreseen her every move, and simply outmaneuvered her. The aftermath of defeat left a foul taste in her mouth—more poignant than the swollen side of her face.

Since anything was for hire in the Barbary Coast, she would start there, combing the doctors, dentists, and back alley butchers who didn't ask questions of their customers. Someone was bound to have noticed a one-eyed ox named Cox and an Irishman with a hole in his side. The rub would be getting them to talk.

35

The Huntress

THURSDAY, JANUARY 4, 1900
PRESENT DAY

CAPTAIN W. LONG STAGGERED out of the dive, drunk on cheap whiskey and women. His billfold was empty.

Commercial Street teemed with lights. Music pushed at the bricks, laughter mingled with shouts, and brawls surged like the ocean's surf. A gunshot pierced the din. No one on the street paid the pop any heed. Drunken men continued staggering from dance hall to peep show, sampling flesh of every color. As unconcerned as they were over a gunshot, none of them paid any mind to the youth leaning against the brick front of *The Lively Flea*.

Isobel huddled in her thick peacoat, waiting and observing. A thin line of smoke seeped from between her lips.

The morning headlines repeated over and over in her mind like a confused gramophone:

ISOBEL KINGSTON MURDERED!
Bereaved husband offers reward.

Captain Long's cap bobbed beneath the bright light. She flicked the cigarette onto the street, pushed off the wall, and followed at a safe distance. As drunk as he appeared, she doubted precaution was necessary, but she wasn't willing to take chances. Not after days of searching, of enduring one false lead after another.

The number of stabbings and eye injuries in the Barbary Coast was astounding. Slowly, through hours of roaming dangerous streets and careful questioning, three names had emerged from the jumble: Johnny Cox, Sam Quinn, and Captain Long. The first two, the one-eyed ox and slim Irishman, were known denizens of the underworld. And the latter was simply a man of opportunity. As it happened, so was Isobel.

If she were lucky, the captain would lead her to his associates. And then what? Her brows drew together in thought.

The Colt Storekeeper she had purchased sat reassuringly in her pocket. One way or another, she would find the answers she sought.

The door to a dance hall flew open, spitting out a group of sailors adrift in a cloud of tobacco smoke. Isobel sidestepped the group, glancing through the gap. Her eyes lingered on the dancing, the music, and the women who fleeced men's pockets with coy smiles and drink. Was that to be her fate?

She pushed the thought aside, and turned her attention back to the meandering Captain Long. Two women, their blouses open, skirts pinned up, faces painted to cover the sorrow of their lives, pawed her peacoat.

"Fancy a Frenchie?" one of the women cooed. "Only a quarter for a lick." Isobel slipped between them, but not before one snatched her cap with a shrill laugh. She grabbed her hat from the woman's hand, smoothed back her short black hair, and flashed the woman a smile before hurrying after Captain Long.

After taking command of the *Pagan Lady*, she had taken every precaution. She was good and truly dead and wanted to remain so. The loss of her hair was only one sacrifice in a well that deepened by the day.

Water gathered on her shoulders from a soft mist that was falling elegantly past the lights. The moon was shadowed. Brooding clouds gathered, blown in from the sea. The street was emptying, not owing to the weather, but rather to a lack of lights and brothels. Captain Long walked towards the docks.

Isobel slowed. The street was close to empty. Soon she would attract attention. No matter how drunk a man, a lone figure trailing after was sure to draw his notice. As if sensing his pursuer, Captain Long turned a corner, disappearing down a narrow lane. On quick, silent feet, she trotted forward, hand slipping inside her pocket. She stopped at the edge of a warehouse. Cautiously, she peeked into the pitch lane. Slurred singing echoed off bricks.

"*Ol' captain Baker, how do you store yer cargo.*" The shadow spread his feet, facing the wall. "*Roll boys! Roll boys, roll!*" Isobel sighed with relief. The man was fumbling with his trouser buttons. "*Some I stow for'ard, boys, an' some I stow a'ter, way high, Miss Sally Brown.*"

A steady stream of urine accompanied his bawdy

shanty. Isobel's fingers curled around her revolver grip. She was, after all, a woman of opportunity. And there was no better opportunity then catching a man with his trousers down.

"She's lovely on the foreyard, an' she's lovely down below boys —"

Taking a deep breath, Isobel plunged into the alley, drawing her Storekeeper. She jammed the business end against the captain's ribs. "Move and you won't be pretty down below." The voice that emerged from her throat was rough and deep, a voice she had used more than once in her unconventional youth.

The captain jerked in alarm. Piss splattered down his trouser leg. Isobel planted a hand on his back and pushed him against the brick. "Hands on the wall."

He did as she ordered. "I don't have no cash." Fear sobered him—his voice was high and clear.

Isobel made no reply. She patted his coat and trousers, emptying them of their contents, and relieving him of his clasp knife. The 'Tickler' was a fine, bone-handled blade. She slipped blade and billfold in her pockets. "Where are your friends, Captain Long?"

"Don't know what yer on about."

"Cox and Quinn."

"Never 'eard hide nor hair of 'em." Clearly, the revolver barrel had lost its effectiveness. She drew the knife, thumbed open the blade, and reached around his front with her left hand. Long rose on his toes with a shrill sound.

"They ain't no friends o' mine."

"You helped them abduct Isobel Kingston."

"I didn't!"

"Quiet," she growled in warning, twitching her wrist.

The man began to quiver with fear.

"They needed a boat," he gulped. "I ain't seen 'em since. God's honest truth." He removed his hand from the wall, and she pressed the blade into a tender spot.

"Stay."

The captain reconsidered his movement, tracing a quick cross on the wall instead of his breast.

"The Lord won't help you," she whispered. "You dumped Isobel Kingston in the bay."

"I didn't," he stammered. "Look, the Kingston girl jumped into the water. Wasn't no murder involved."

"The police found a body."

"Quinn hatched up a scheme after they lost the girl. He wanted his payload. They went and got a second girl that looked just like the first."

"Who?"

"Some young tart at *Cowboy's Rest.*"

"Why'd they kill her, then?"

"The headlines—about the ransom. Scared 'em witless I s'pose."

The words hit her like a slap in the face. Her blade faltered.

"I swear it. I was just pilotin' the boat."

"Who hired them to abduct her?"

"Hired? How the hell should I know?"

Isobel thought furiously, considering her next move. She couldn't release the man, but neither could she hand him over to the police without revealing her living state. And haircut or no, her male disguise wouldn't bear scrutiny. Her brother Lotario could barely pass as a man. At best, she passed as a sixteen year old boy, hardly credible, and hardly enough to inspire fear. Unfortunately, more than fear was needed. Should she let him go, the captain might recognize her as the woman who'd leapt overboard.

"Where is your boat?" she asked.

"Off of Front, at Fisherman's Wharf."

"Button up your trousers," she ordered, withdrawing the knife and thumbing it shut.

Long trembled over the buttoning process. When the task was complete, she gripped his arm, pressing the Store-keeper into his ribs. "If you run, I'll shoot, but if you take me to your boat, we'll sit down and discuss a proposition. There's a reward out for Cox and Quinn. If you cooperate, I might be persuaded to forget your name, and share part of it. Savvy?"

The captain's body tensed, like a hound catching a scent. She imagined his eyes widening as possibilities tumbled around in his empty head. She wondered if he had read the morning headlines, or if, in fact, he could read at all.

Whatever revelations and possibilities were spinning in his addled brain, Captain Long led the way to his berth without fuss or fight.

36

Becomes the Hunted

THE WHARF WAS QUIET. A distant light spun in hypnotic circles on the rock guarding the Golden Gate. Rain spattered the dingy cobblestones, pattering on the planks, and rocking boats on their moor lines.

A bitter wind swept from the sea, past twin points into the sheltered bay. It sliced through the gaps between buildings, through the fibers of Isobel's wool coat, and straight through her bones. By the time they reached the docks her clothes were damp.

A forest of masts swayed in the restless harbor, creaking and whispering with worry. The wharf was vacant, save for a few passing shadows. Captain Long stomped down the dock, passing feluccas, trawlers, and cutters. Ironically, her own boat, the *Pagan Lady*, was moored in the bay, not three piers away.

Waves slapped at the pilings. The surf rose, tossing spiteful white caps at the sea wall. A storm was brewing.

"She's right down 'ere." Captain Long pointed. "Rum awaits."

The last thing Long needed was more rum. Perhaps not, she silently corrected. Drink might loosen his tongue.

Captain Long's trawler was sandwiched between two others, all nearly identical. The boats fought for space along the docks, hulls bumping with the waves, tugging on their moorings.

Long stepped over the rail and into his trawler, stumbling over the forgotten drop. Before he could recover, Isobel stepped up and over, dropping to the deck with a wince. The world blurred, and tilted. She gritted her teeth, turning pain to anger, and grabbed Long's collar. It was fortunate she did.

Two shadows detached themselves from the helm. "Ahoy there, Cap'n." A familiar Irish lilt cooed in the night. The round end of a cigar glowed in the dark.

Dread stole the breath from Isobel's lungs. She tensed, pulling Long near, as the Ox loomed closer.

"Quinn!" Long slurred in friendly surprise. "We was jus' talking 'bout the two of you."

"Fancy that," said Quinn. "And just who is 'we'?" Isobel pressed the revolver between Long's ribs in warning, as if the nickel could pierce wool and flesh.

"This lad and I, a' course."

"Yer new cabin boy looks scared witless," Cox rumbled.

"Don't know why," Long drawled casually. "The boy has a barrel to me ribs."

Isobel transferred her revolver from his ribs to temple. "Stay back," she rasped, and to Long, she muttered, "Bastard."

"At your pleasure." The Irishman chuckled. "It'll save us the trouble."

Isobel's heart thudded against her breast. Her throat went dry as realization sparked her mind. Cox and Quinn weren't taking chances with a reward out for their heads. They had come to snip the remaining thread.

A shift of movement was the only warning she had. Light pierced the night. An explosion, a zip, and a fine, warm mist. The man in front of her staggered, gurgling, sagging. Cox charged, blade in hand.

Isobel pushed her dying captive at the larger man. It slowed him, but didn't stop. Steel pierced flesh, burning up her arm. Remembering her revolver, she squeezed the trigger, firing blindly. Air whipped past her cheek. The men moved impossibly slow. Sound dampened, blood rushed in her ears.

Isobel scrambled towards an adjoining boat, hopped up and over the rail, landed hard on the deck and shot forward, clambering over the next. She leapt onto the dock, boots beating against the planks.

Lanterns bobbed ahead. Distant shouts. She cut across a jam of boats, leaping from one rail to the next, balancing on a maze of bobbing perches. The revolver was warm in her hand, slick with blood. Rain beat against her face, coldness mingling with warm salt.

She reached another dock. Sound rushed back into her ears. Shouting, running, more gunshots. Lanterns wavered in the wind. And Isobel ran. She slipped through a gap between warehouses, into darkness and cover, and then burst out the other side with the wind at her back.

The voices fell behind, the lights faded, and still she ran. Air fluttered like a hummingbird in her lungs. Panic seared her veins. Blindly, she raced.

Fear had triumphed.

The thought struck her, flashed in her mind. She forced herself to stop in the shadow of a dock house. Fighting for air, she gazed down the docks, squinting past the drizzle towards the *Pagan Lady*. The cutter's familiar outline tossed in the agitated waters. All was dark.

Isobel could not breathe. The harder she tried to calm her racing heart, the faster it sped. Craving movement, she let her legs carry her down a ladder, and into a dinghy she had secured to a piling. Her hands shook. She fumbled with the oars, and then heaved, rowing with a slice in her ribs.

Safety, safety, her mind screamed. She had been an utter fool. And Long had signed his own death warrant. The jerk of his body had traveled along her fingers as surely as Quinn's bullet from its barrel. The spray of blood, hot and salty, covered her face. She spat into the water. And put her back into the oars.

Wood knocked against wood. Surprised, she drew the oars in, peeling her palms from the handles. With clumsy fingers, she secured the dinghy to the boat, and climbed onboard, dropping to the deck with relief. The deck shifted, narrowed, a tunnel of blackness danced at the edges of her sight. Warmth oozed down her face. The boat lurched. Or was it her quaking?

A shadow moved, her hackles rose, and so did her arm. She spun, revolver in hand. A streak of silver snapped forward. Something hard and unyielding struck her wrist. The Colt clattered to the ground.

A strong hand gripped her wrist, twisting her arm. With a thud, her knees hit the deck, followed by stomach, and cheek. An unyielding weight dug into her back.

Isobel screamed in pain.

37

A Shadow in the Fog

THE SCREAM WAS SOFT. A strangled whimper that accomplished more than a blow to the face. Isobel's attacker jerked back in surprise, easing the pressure off her spine. The moment he relaxed, she reached for her fallen revolver. With snaking precision, her foe snatched it off the deck, and took a step back.

"Surprise I expected, but hardly a gun," a voice drawled in the night, deep and reverberating. His greeting was far from reassuring. She twisted, and scrambled backwards, until her shoulders hit the brief bulwark.

"Mrs. Kingston, I presume?"

Isobel stared at the stranger in shock. His features were obscured by the brim of a homburg and his body by a long coat that was collecting rain. Silver glinted in the night—near his eyes and hand. Spectacles, her mind supplied.

And her throbbing wrist told her the latter was a walking stick.

Water dripped off his brim, pattering on the deck. Slowly, painfully, she gripped the rail and pulled herself to an upright position, swaying with the rocking boat. She wiped the water from her eyes and the stranger bent to recover her fallen cap.

"Atticus Riot," the man introduced himself without ceremony, holding her hat out to her. "You appear to be injured, Mrs. Kingston."

"Do not call me by that name," she growled, ignoring the offering. It was pointless to roughen her voice. Somehow, this man knew she was alive, and had tracked her to her boat.

"You're quite right," he said. "We've not been introduced. May I ask after the name you have chosen for your after life?"

"Call me Bel," she stated. "One *E*, one *L*."

"Pleased to meet you, Miss Bel." Amusement tinted his words. "Shall we head below deck? You appear on the verge of collapse."

"I am perfectly fine," she lied. "My Colt, if you please, Mr. Riot."

The man regarded her in silence. A gust of wind nipped at his homburg. Isobel's teeth knocked together. At length, he tucked stick and cap under his arm, and reached into a pocket. The brim of his hat dipped as he opened the cylinder and ejected the cartridges into the palm of his hand. After pocketing the ammunition, he held the useless weapon out to her.

Isobel glared at the man. She snatched her revolver for principle's sake.

"Ladies first, but if you would prefer, I'll make an

exception in this instance, Miss Bel."

"Did Kingston send you?" she demanded.

"Alex Kingston hired my detective agency to find you," Riot answered truthfully. "However, I'm no longer in your husband's employ." His voice was everything opposite of the storm, of the restless sea and mournful wind. He was like a shadow in the fog. Unfortunately, whether he was risk or haven, she did not know. She could only stand, chattering with cold and fear, clutching her useless revolver.

"I don't expect you to trust me, Miss Bel," he said, following her thoughts. "There's nothing I can say here to convince you otherwise, but we do have other matters to discuss. I'll be in the saloon if you decide to join me." The man turned towards the hatch.

Isobel always preferred to have the initiative, not the other way around. She briefly considered throwing her empty revolver at the back of his head. But it seemed a childish gesture—better to knock him over the head when he descended the companionway ladder.

Intending to do just that, she stepped forward, but her legs were uncooperative. Instead, she stumbled and fell.

38

A Damsel in Distress

THE SOFT THUD STALLED Riot in his tracks. He paused at the hatch and squinted over the cabin top. Tossing his stick inside the saloon, he stepped back on deck. Before Isobel could offer protest, he gripped her under the arms and hoisted her upright, wrapping an arm around her waist. Her wiry body tensed beneath his hand. A wince. Careful of her ribs, he walked her to the hatch, and assisted her down the companionway ladder.

"I'm fine," she muttered in the darkness, brushing off his hold to collapse on the settee berth.

"Only a stumble," he agreed, striking a match. Riot steadied the swaying oil lamp with one hand and lit it with the other. A warm, soft glow chased back the darkness. The cabin of mahogany and oak was foggy. He removed his spectacles, wiped the glass dry on a handkerchief and replaced the wire. His gaze fell on Isobel.

Despite the boyish haircut, black dye, blood, mottled bruises, and exhaustion, the striking bone structure he had first observed remained, naming her Lotario's twin sister. She was bleeding from her forehead and blood rolled down her left hand, dripping onto the fabric. The sleeve of her coat had been sliced. She was fighting the urge to lie down, mightily resisting, and slowly losing the battle of will.

Riot clenched his jaw, flicking the match into an ashtray, before kneeling beside the berth. First, he examined her head and then her arm. "You were cut."

"No," she corrected, "I blocked a blade with my arm. The men responsible have likely dug themselves another hole to hide in."

Gently, he eased her out of her coat. Blood saturated the sleeve of her shirt. He probed the torn fabric, gazing at the flesh beneath. A long gash trailed up her forearm.

Isobel surrendered to gravity, cheek resting heavily on the cushion. He sat on the berth, unhooked a wooden cufflink, and carefully rolled her sleeve over the wound.

Riot felt her eyes on him. His fingers stilled, and he met her gaze—they glowed amber in the lantern light.

"I was going to knock you over the head with my revolver," she whispered.

"I expected no less of you, Miss Bel."

"All I needed was to see you in the light, Mr. Riot."

"And what have you determined?" he asked.

"Your weakness."

Danger lurked in her voice. His eyes traveled from her own, down her body, to her right hand. She held an open clasp knife, poised to pierce his ribs.

Riot ignored the blade. "What of yours, Miss Bel?"

She swallowed. "I'll let you know as soon as I discover one." Eyes flashed with arrogance, and she flicked the knife closed.

The edge of his lip twitched. "Well played."

"I have my moments," she said, even as a long shiver seized her body. Not all of her ploy had been an act. Shock and exhaustion were taking their toll.

"I'm afraid your arm will need sewing."

"Better my arm than my throat."

"I should like a full account."

"As payment for your medical services?"

"If you like."

"It depends on the neatness of your stitch."

"Agreed." He cinched a temporary bandage around her arm, stood, and retrieved a medicinal bottle from the small galley cupboard. "I suggest you drink a good portion of this."

She accepted the bottle, shimmied herself upright, loosened tie and collar, and took a long draught. As Riot busied himself with the paraffin stove in the galley, Isobel sat quietly, alternating between drinking and watching the detective move confidently through her cabin.

A book she had been reading and the newspaper declaring her death had been disturbed. The latter had a set of new creases and the former had been moved from its previous location on the headboard shelf. Obviously, Riot had been waiting some time for her arrival. "I see you've made yourself comfortable," she said to his narrow back.

"I required answers," he replied. "And I should add," Riot glanced at her out of the corner of his eye, "I was beginning to worry. Had I known you were involved in a gun fight only three docks down, I would have joined you sooner. Since I've only just realized you are alive, I would hardly like to lose you again."

"I prefer to remain dead."

"I'm sure the young woman whose body washed ashore would gladly switch places with you." The words hit her like a kick to the stomach.

Isobel froze. Every bruise and slice, the long days of searching, the fear and strife, came rushing back to her body. She closed her eyes, suddenly exhausted. "It was my foolish letters," she whispered.

The quiet words lingered in the cabin, accompanied by the creak of wood and the swaying lantern. When the stove began radiating warmth, Riot filled the large brass kettle with fresh water from the boat's stores and set it on top.

"Indirectly, yes," he said at length, sitting on the berth beside her. The young woman's bruised face was etched with pain. "But I suspect you had good reason for writing your own ransom demand."

Isobel turned her eyes towards the hull.

The only sound she made as Riot disinfected the gash with stinging brandy and applied his sewing skills to her flesh, was a slurred murmur, "I should have planned for such an eventuality." Her words were laden with regret.

39

The Detective

A RICH, HEADY AROMA seduced Isobel's eyes open. The boat was calm, gently rolling with lazy swells. The womb of the *Pagan Lady* was warm and cozy. A bright drizzle swirled outside the open porthole. Cold air brushed her cheek. Moving seemed an extraordinary feat.

Isobel lowered the heavy wool blanket, blinking at the saloon. The Shipmate stove radiated heat, a coffee percolator sat cooling in the galley, and her peacoat hung on a hook drying. There was no sign of the detective. Panic propelled her out of the berth. She stumbled, gritted her teeth, and clambered up the companionway.

The docks had been washed clean, and now they relaxed under a soothing grey. White sails skimmed the distant waters, fishermen milled around their boats, and Isobel scanned her own, twisting towards the aft. Her heart stilled, and she felt foolish. Atticus Riot sat on the cabin trunk, sipping his coffee, watching the wharves. Formally dressed as he was, he made the *Pagan Lady* look like the Palace Hotel.

Isobel was suddenly aware of her own state: open collar, rolled up cuff, a bandaged arm, and boyish hair sticking in all directions.

"Good morning, Mr. Riot," she said primly, drawing herself up.

He stood, and removed his hat, inclining his head. "Good morning, Miss Bel. I trust you slept well?"

"I did, thank you."

"Are my stitches satisfactory?"

Isobel glanced at her bandaged arm. "I'll inspect them and let you know shortly." She disappeared down the companionway.

A half an hour later, she returned, scrubbed and presentable in a clean shirt, tie, and sweater. She joined him on the cabin trunk, at a safe distance, facing the bay towards Alcatraz. The mug of coffee warmed her hands and sharpened her brain.

Isobel braced herself for a barrage of questions, but the detective never asked. He seemed content to wait, calm and sure as a crag in a storm-tossed sea. As if sitting on a stolen cutter with a woman dressed as a boy, whose death certificate had been signed, was an everyday occurrence.

She studied his profile. Riot was not a large man, but she could feel his presence. He was the kind of man she would notice in a crowded room. The grey that peppered his trim beard betrayed his age, and his silver spectacles lent him a scholarly air, but she knew better than to be deceived. The walking stick resting beside his leg was a solid reminder that the man was quick as a snake.

"Are you blind without your spectacles?" she inquired, breaking the mounting silence.

Riot tapped a finger on the side of his mug. The question had caught him off guard; however he answered smoothly enough. "Nearly." He removed his hat, set it aside, and smoothed his hair into order with quick proficiency. She eyed the slash of white hair at his right temple.

"Do you generally shoot first and ask later?"

"It has served me well thus far," she replied. "Do you make a habit of ambushing women on their property?"

"Stolen property," he pointed out. "And I'm afraid I must admit to making a habit of such things, but then, that's a detective's lot."

"At least you're honest," she remarked dryly.

"Not always."

Isobel laughed, a sharp, unladylike outburst that she quickly stifled. Laughter had become unfamiliar, and at the moment it aggravated her bruised body. She sipped her coffee, gathering her thoughts.

"I have the distinct feeling that you are waiting for me to begin my narrative," she said at length.

"I'm a patient man, Miss Bel."

"I don't think you are, Mr. Riot." Silver eyes pierced him, like a hawk about to swoop. "You're a confident man. One who wields silence like that stick of yours."

"My gambit appears lost on you," Riot noted.

"I keep my cards close."

"A deal is a deal."

"As they say in chess, you have the initiative."

"I'm hardly threatening you."

"No, but you still have the bullets with which to ruin

me." Isobel stood, attempting to hide her stiffness. "I'm hungry." She disappeared below deck.

Since sunrise, not three docks away, official-looking men had been moving along the wharves, centered around a trawler. The same dock where gunshots had been fired the night before. Riot continued to watch the police investigation as he mulled over their exchange of words. And then his gaze traveled southward, towards Nob Hill. Stories bubbled on the surface, but secrets dwelt below. He suspected Miss Bel had been collecting secrets her entire life.

After a time, when the thumping in the galley had subsided, Riot picked up Isobel's abandoned mug and joined her in the saloon. She sat on one of the two berths that doubled as a settee. A plate of salted beef, preserves, and biscuits sat in the center of the narrow table.

Riot set down the mugs, hung his hat on a hook, and shed his coat. He rested his stick against the wall.

"More coffee?"

"Please."

"As uncomfortable as it might be," he began, refilling their cups, "I'd greatly appreciate you confiding in me." He set her mug on the table, and settled himself opposite. "The men who abducted you, a Captain Long, and two others, one Irish and a large fellow built like an ox—"

"Captain W. Long," Isobel inserted. "I do believe he is dead. The other two, who murdered him and tried to shoot me last night, go by the name of Johnny Cox and Sam Quinn."

Riot paused, poised to drink. He looked over the rim at her, and slowly set down his mug. "I'm surprised you are alive, Miss Bel."

"The physician said that very same thing about me, to

my mother the day I was born. I was too stubborn to die then, and I'm too stubborn now. You were saying?"

"The men paid Old Sue a whole fifty cents to deliver the ransom demand to your father. Since the path to your family home is steep, Old Sue paid a little girl a penny to run the letter up to the front porch."

Isobel's fingers worried over a biscuit.

"The men doubled back to sweep their trail after—I assume you escaped?"

She dipped her chin. "Long received a knot on his head. Cox lost an eye in the process and I put a hole in Quinn's side. I nearly drowned. They killed Old Sue, didn't they?" she asked hoarsely.

"With a lethal dose of laudanum in an Old Tom bottle."

"And the little girl?"

"Even though she saw them, and was able to name the boat, she escaped their notice. I have an agent watching the girl."

A shudder of relief traveled through Isobel's body. Her hands disappeared inside the too long sleeves of her sweater, and she sat back, staring forlornly at the ruins of her biscuit.

"There are times, Miss Bel," he began calmly, "when laying your cards on the table is the wisest course. Failing to do so at the proper time generally ends in bloodshed. I would like you to consider the table from my vantage point."

Isobel looked from her plate to his face.

"You disappeared for nearly two hours before you boarded the ferry. You visited your brother, stole proof of ownership to his cutter, and then you were abducted—or so you claim."

"I'm not making a claim," she snapped.

"Hear me out," he said firmly. "You intended to study Law, did you not?"

She nodded in reply.

"How would events hold up in court? You claim you escaped, yet you didn't go to the police. You disappeared. You sent ransom demands to three newspapers. Who's to say you didn't hire Cox and Quinn yourself?"

"Because I didn't."

"Might it become your word against theirs and a mountain of incriminating circumstance?"

Isobel's lips pressed together. There was truth in his words.

"Let's consider the rest of your actions. You cut and dyed your hair, dressed in male attire, roamed unsavory streets—" Riot paused, rubbing a hand over his beard, eyes alight with realization. "That's how you tracked your abductors—by their injuries. You questioned the doctors in the Barbary Coast."

"It took too long."

"But you were successful."

"Things didn't end as I planned."

"Things rarely do," he said, offering her a smile.

"That's not very reassuring," she sighed. "I can fill in the rest. I lured 'some young tart' from a brothel, dressed her in my clothing, and dumped her overboard to complete my ruse. Since Captain Long was a witness, I needed to silence him as well. There was a gunfight. I arrived at my boat covered in blood, a spent casing in my revolver." She gestured towards his pocket. "Ordinarily, I would think a jury mad to believe such a story, but not with the graft that would likely change hands."

"Nor with your unconventional reputation. You're in a

precarious position."

"I've been in one far longer than I care to ponder."

"Alex Kingston." At the sound of her husband's name, fury flashed across her eyes.

"You appear to have all the pieces to my puzzle."

"On the contrary, I'm missing a very important piece," he admitted. "The why of it."

"Because I'm a daft fool," she whispered.

"I don't take you for a fool, Miss Bel."

"Well, I am."

"You're only a fool when you make a mistake at my age."

"You don't strike me as a man who makes mistakes, Mr. Riot."

"Frequently and grandly," he admitted with a self-deprecating smile.

A knot inside of her unwound, and for the first time in a long while, she decided to trust. "I'll allow you to retract your statement after you've heard the whole of my story."

40

A Caged Bird

"As you so delicately phrased it, I have an unconventional reputation. Society has no place for a spirited woman, unless that woman happens to be charming. And I am not charming."

"You are something else entirely," he agreed. She narrowed her eyes. Riot leaned back and crossed his legs, folding his hands.

"My father was indulgent, but he finally took note when I was fifteen. Lotario, Merrik, and I, along with some of their friends, were roaming the saloons. We drew the attention of the police. And out of the entire group, I was the only one arrested for disorderly conduct, because I was a woman posing as a man. Curtis, my older brother who works in the city, was able to keep my name out of the newspapers. However, I was sent abroad with a respectable spinster, and forced into a young lady's school in Dresden.

"Largely owing to my desperation to leave the school, I surprised everyone and graduated with honors. I convinced my chaperone to travel. As it turned out, she was not as responsible as my father believed. She ran off on some lark of her own, abandoning me for a slick Italian. I'd like to think I drove her to insanity. Needless to say, I made ample use of my new-found freedom."

"Your father said you were living with a fencer and an artist, which incidentally, was what led me to Lotario. Your brother said the truth was far worse than what your father believed. With what precisely were you occupying yourself, Miss Bel?"

"My activities in Venice have nothing to do with this current situation," Isobel replied firmly. Her answer only fueled his curiosity. She sipped her coffee, eyes sliding to the right, to the row of books on the small shelf.

"Fernando dragged me home in shame, or so my parents hoped. Fortunately, I've never been the shamed type."

Riot plucked one of the books from the shelf. And Isobel faltered. He turned *The Adventures of Sherlock Holmes* over in his hand.

"Am I that transparent to you, Mr. Riot?"

"Nothing more than a lucky guess, I assure you," he said dryly.

"I'm less than reassured."

"Investigating a murder?"

Isobel huffed. "A stolen piece of art. And in Austria I solved a string of dairy cow thefts, if you must know." Color rose in her cheeks. "I was working my way up to murder."

"Scandalous." Riot's eyes twinkled with amusement.

"As I was saying," Isobel cleared her throat. "I returned to California, and again Curtis had to hush the newspapers on my behalf. There was only rumor left, but there is *always* rumor. Unfortunately, I soon learned that my father's business pursuits were failing. The family holdings were in jeopardy. It seemed strange—both the vineyards and shipyards at the same time. The more I looked into it, the more suspicious things became. One coincidence after another. And I do not trust coincidence.

"So last summer, I joined San Francisco's society as a transformed young woman: a newly emerged butterfly out of her cocoon." Isobel's voice dripped with sarcasm. "Despite my loathing of the lady's school, I had come away with valuable resources. I charmed my way up the social ladder, until I began mingling with the likes of Kingston and his ilk—railway investors and mine owners—whose wives and daughters were possessed of flapping tongues. Through one tedious social affair after another, along with rumor and scandal, a disturbing picture began to form around one man: Alex Kingston, a very successful lawyer with a flourishing legal firm. The type of man who gets exactly what he desires, but more importantly, so do his clients."

"Such as Thomas Wade."

"I see you've been thorough."

"In all things. Your father recently sold the property for your ransom."

"I suspected as much. Thomas Wade has been coveting Father's property in Napa for years. Father is not a businessman, but a sentimental man who places value on heritage. The boatbuilding company in Sausalito and the vineyards in Napa are like children to him; he wouldn't sell, no matter the price."

"Which is when men turn to Kingston."

"Precisely," she nodded. "I don't know if you recall the battle in Sausalito seven years ago, between the hill people and the flatlanders?"

"The former wished to put sewer lines and street lamps in town."

"And the flatlanders were content with the way things were, because bringing civilization to the waterfront would increase taxes."

"A fire swayed the vote."

"Wiping out the majority of Water Street and the voices of dissent," she continued. "There was rumor of arson, but nothing ever came of it. I wasn't surprised to learn that the majority of Kingston's clients own property in the Sausalito hills. And you may remember the feud on Nob Hill, between Michael Norton and the lowly milk man Noah Hall?"

"A bit before your time, Miss Bel," Riot said.

"I spent long hours in Curtis' offices researching legal transactions and newspaper archives when I wasn't plastering a smile on my face and pretending to dote on the latest Parisian fashion." She ran her fingers through her hair, managing to muss rather than tame the uneven mop.

"I do recall the battle of egos clearly. Norton wanted the entire block for himself, but Hall refused to sell."

"And unlike the Crocker versus Yung feud, where Crocker built a forty foot fence around the poor man's house, Norton turned to Kingston. Hall had an unfortunate accident a month later while driving his milk wagon."

"An advantageous accident for Norton."

"It appeared to be an accident, but when you add it to a long list of similar accidents, Kingston's clients begin to appear uncommonly lucky."

"All circumstantial."

"And not all ending in death." Her lip twisted ruefully. "The variety of schemes makes events difficult to connect."

"Unless you're looking for a pattern."

Isobel nodded. "I had no way to prove my suspicions, and what was more, I began receiving marriage proposals from hopeful suitors. Many of whom were wealthy. Somehow, I attracted Kingston's attention, but unlike the others, I could not immediately rebuff his offers. I needed to get close to him, to learn all I could. To stave off the other suitors, I enrolled at university.

"Unfortunately, in the months that followed, my father's business—and the future of my brothers—suffered one disaster after another. For the first time in Father's life, he was forced to turn to creditors. Out of desperation, I decided to confront Kingston. I claimed that I had proof of his meddling. And if he did not desist, I would take the information to the newspapers."

Riot arched a brow.

"It was utterly foolish, I know." Her voice lowered to a whisper. "Absolutely naive of me."

"You didn't tell your father?"

"I told Curtis," she protested. "He told me I was reading too many dime novels. But even if Curtis had believed me, there was no way to prove it, and even if there had been a way, one does not clash with Alex Kingston."

"How did Kingston respond when you confronted him?"

"He told me to send the information to the newspapers, that he had them in his pocket. And then he mentioned the Book of Job, the verse where his sons and daughters were killed."

"*Thy sons and thy daughters were eating and drinking wine in their eldest brother's house,*" Riot recited, sonorously. "*And behold, there came a great wind from the wilderness, and smote the four corners of the house, and it fell upon the young men, and they are dead.*"

"Yes, that very verse." Isobel shivered, as if that great wind had touched her neck. "My bluff had failed miserably, but worse, I was exposed—and powerless. I determined to apply myself at university while keeping an eye on Kingston's affairs. Sooner or later, he would make a mistake. I didn't hear from him for weeks. That is, until he called on me at university.

"Kingston had an offer—a marriage proposal. As a wedding gift, he would see to it that my father's business efforts flourished, and in return, I would pass on any pertinent gossip I gleaned from the wives and daughters of Kingston's associates."

"And if you didn't?"

"Not only would things continue as they had been with my family's business, but the events that Curtis had taken pains to silence would come to light. My reputation would be ruined, and since I was now part of society, my family would be dragged into the resulting scandal."

"Blackmail."

"At its very best." Isobel gazed at a distant point, somewhere far beyond the wooden hull. "Kingston likes to control people, Mr. Riot. In his younger days he enjoyed breaking in wild horses. The more spirited the pony, the more satisfaction it gave him. He's not a kind man."

Riot clutched his coffee, knuckles white.

"As hopeless as it appeared, I saw an opportunity." Isobel's eyes glittered dangerously, surprising Riot for a second time. "I feigned helplessness, terror, an unwilling compliance, and I married him on my 20th birthday, becoming as pliable and boring as any other dithering society woman. Not only did I deny Kingston the satisfaction of breaking me, but what was more, I was in a perfect position to dig deeper into his affairs."

"At an unacceptable price," Riot said. The words were nearly a growl, and Isobel tilted her head, studying the man across from her in a new light.

"No more than most women pay," she stated. "It took everything I had not to gut him, but I had won, despite his —manipulations." The edge of her lip curved with satisfaction.

"You sound as if victory is paramount. Surely your well-being is of higher concern?"

"Oh, I don't know about all that," Isobel said lightly. "As a little girl, I ended up bruised and battered trying to outdo my brothers. A victory was always well worth the pain."

Riot swallowed his outrage.

"Alex forgot one very important thing. As his wife, his reputation was now tied to mine. He could hardly expose my past without bringing attention upon himself, and a man like Kingston must always remain in the shadows. He sought to tame me, and it was only after our marriage that he realized a wild animal had been waiting to be invited inside his camp.

"At the same time, my position was precarious at best. I was now an unwanted wife who had made it a point to know his business associates and his enemies. Kingston still controlled the center of the chess board. It was only a matter of time before I'd be backed into a corner and some accident befell me. I saw but one strategy."

"To disappear."

"Not just disappear, Mr. Riot, but to die," she corrected. "Only death would save my family and me."

"Your family is still at risk, Miss Bel."

"All the evidence I have against Kingston involves a pattern of success and a list of wealthy businessmen who pay him a monthly retainer for nonexistent legal services. But surely his society wife's death would garner attention? It's nothing significant by itself, but imagine if her family's business interests should take another turn for the worse shortly after her tragic death?"

Riot smoothed his beard in thought. "The newspapers would relish the unfortunate suffering of a family in mourning. In such a situation, an accusation would carry more weight."

"Precisely." She nodded, pleased that he was following so readily. "Small bribes to lumber yards, a whispered word of warning in a buyer's ear, and an orchestration of an occasional equipment failure at a vineyard—those things are inconspicuous. But constant tragedy paints another picture."

"It was still a gamble."

"One I had to take," she said, tightly. "I couldn't tolerate another moment under Kingston's roof."

"Understandable."

"Regardless, I was outmaneuvered," she added bitterly. "I was intending to force the issue with Kingston, by visiting my family no matter his protest. But I couldn't simply storm out of his house; things had become more complicated. Even before our marriage, Kingston had assigned men to shadow me, and I suspected my correspondence was being monitored as well. To make the necessary arrangements, I would need to shake my shadows. During the Christmas party, I slipped away and sabotaged a carriage spring so I would have an excuse to take a hack."

"And the warehouse fire?"

"An unexpected gift, or so I thought. I didn't have to defy Kingston to visit my family after all. He very conveniently left."

"You slipped out, lost your shadows, and walked to your brother's establishment where you stole his proof of ownership to a yacht he had never sailed."

"And then I walked to the berth, and stowed money, papers, and clothes on the *Pagan Lady*, intending to make use of her at a later date. Lotario had built a number of cleverly concealed compartments into his vessel."

Riot scanned the saloon. During the course of his original search, he had failed to discover a secret compartment. His cursory glance revealed nothing new. When his gaze returned to Isobel, her eyes held mischief, picking up the light of her dark blue sweater.

"I suspect he had plans to conceal his lovers," she confided. "It's a vessel worthy of smugglers."

"I'll keep that in mind during my next invasion of your stolen vessel."

"Some warning would be appreciated next time. I'd hate to shoot you."

"But bashing me over the head is acceptable?"

"I never make promises, Mr. Riot."

"Noted."

"Anyhow, my scheme was simple: I planned to go sailing, as I did before Europe, alone on one of my father's yachts. I was going to run her into a cliff. It would appear to be an unfortunate boating accident by a foolhardy young woman. The lack of a body wouldn't raise an eyebrow—the sea has swallowed many a soul. And if Kingston had shown up on my family's doorstep, demanding to accompany me, he would have been part of that accident."

"While you swam safely to shore."

"I hoped for the latter scenario. It would have saved me grief."

"But you were abducted."

"On the ferry," Isobel confirmed. "I miscalculated. I think Alex staged the warehouse fire, killing two birds with one stone. It's what he does best. Not only would it give me a chance to leave, but he would collect the insurance money. He was the only one who could predict my actions and plan accordingly. He knew I was set on visiting my family."

"So your father, who was already in debt, would be forced to come up with the ransom money."

"Yes." She frowned. "Which is why I sent the ransom letters to the newspapers. Ransom notes always seem to follow the same outline, don't they? 'No police involved or we'll kill the girl.' By making the abduction public, I hoped that my father would be deterred from gathering ransom funds, and that my abductors would be too scared to try to collect from him after my escape.

"And I don't doubt Alex enjoyed the idea of me in those men's hands." Isobel leaned back on the settee, toying with her short hair. "I wonder——" she murmured.

Anyone else would have asked 'what', but Riot was not everyone, so he watched her think and waited for the thought to surface.

In the ensuing quiet, she looked at him. "I wonder if it wasn't my letters that killed the unfortunate woman after all, but rather my escape. What if Alex had paid Quinn and Cox to kill me, and dump my body on that beach? He would have rid himself of a liability, forced my father to sell his property, *and* collected insurance on the warehouse."

Isobel's words struck a chord. "*That* beach," Riot murmured.

She tilted her head in question.

"Railroad wars, Miss Bel."

"One discarded body hardly constitutes a war."

"The Santa Fe Railway Company is currently building a ferry and railway terminus at the nearby point. The Santa Fe and Pacific Union are old rivals."

Isobel turned his theory over in her mind. She narrowed her eyes, irritated that she had not seen the obvious sooner. "A dead woman on the beach would cause suspicion, and might halt, or at the very least, delay construction."

"Construction delays cost a great deal of money."

"It fits with Kingston's style," agreed Isobel. "And is inconspicuous enough to escape notice. No one would look twice at Kingston and his clients. Who would suspect him of hiring men to kill his own wife and dump her body on a beach to halt construction? It's absurd."

"The police are questioning the laborers at length. They're convinced the culprits are Chinese."

"Isn't there a shrimping village nearby?"

"There is," answered Riot. "The police are tearing the village apart as well. I suspect Kingston has killed a whole flock of birds with one stone."

"How so?"

"The shrimping village, the railway workers, and the warehouse fire all have one thing in common: the Chinese."

"But to what end?"

"The Chinese are prosperous merchants. Vilifying them is always good for everyone's business, save for the

Chinese, especially if someone has their eye on that section of shoreline."

"Well, Alex is efficient, I'll give him that," she muttered. A shiver shook her body and she hugged herself tightly.

An amiable silence fell over the pair, their minds turning over revelations and possibilities. At length, Riot gently knocked a fist against his thigh.

"There is one troubling point."

"Only one?" Isobel asked, wryly.

"When Kingston and your parents came to identify a horribly mutilated corpse at the undertakers, I could have sworn his surprise and anger was genuine. I'm not convinced your husband wanted you dead."

"Perhaps Cox and Quinn didn't follow his orders to the letter, or maybe he knew it wasn't me."

"I sensed genuine grief under the fury."

One slim shoulder raised. "It hardly matters, although I'm surprised my husband bothered with anger, considering I was such a nuisance."

"But were you?"

"I've been a nuisance all my life, Mr. Riot."

"Entirely subjective."

"I'll grant you that."

"You seem to forget that you are an heiress."

Puzzlement shone in her eyes. "Of my mother's home, and a fair amount of money, but nothing compared to Kingston's fortune."

"And property," he reminded.

"Trees and hillside and dairy farms."

"In the 70s there was a ripple of excitement when manganese was discovered in the Sausalito hills—enough to justify small-scale mining."

"But the mines are closed. I used to explore them with Lotario. They would always flood."

"Your family's property is higher than the tunnels. The land has been in your mother's family since the Gold Rush. It appears perfectly untouched and preserved."

"But the land would pass to me, not—" Isobel cut off in realization. "Unless a child were born before I died."

"It seems an elaborate scheme, but if there's valuable metal to be had, it would be well worth the effort."

"And here I thought it was my feigned charm," Isobel mumbled.

"I wouldn't discount your charms entirely, Miss Bel."

"Flattery is lost on me." Moving stiffly, she sat forward and set her mug on the table, then wiped her hands on her trousers. "We need to find Quinn and Cox."

"And the identity of the young woman who was murdered."

Isobel frowned. "Yes, of course." She stood, picked up the plate, and returned it to the galley.

Riot followed her stiff movements. A shudder swept through her body, and she gripped the edge of the counter, dipping her chin and closing her eyes. He stood, and moved behind her. When she turned, her eyes were like the early morning mist.

"Mr. Riot," she said, hoarsely. "Kingston can't know I'm alive."

In answer, he reached into his pocket, and withdrew four cartridges and one brass casing. The cool metal sat in the palm of his hand. An offering of trust. "I'll find another way."

"*We* will find another way," Isobel corrected, plucking the offering from his hand.

"Miss Bel, if you wish to avoid police attention—"

"Whether or not you agree," Isobel interrupted. "I'll follow you anyhow. I always finish what I begin."

"Except university."

Reaching for her Colt, Isobel scowled at the man. She pushed the cartridges into their chambers, and pocketed the casing. He opened his mouth to protest, but Isobel jumped in first. "If you have learned anything during the course of your investigation, then you should know not to argue with me *after* I have a loaded gun." She clicked the cylinder shut.

"You only have four cartridges," he pointed out.

"I'll only need one," she retorted.

"I'd rather not test that assertion."

"Nor would I," she admitted. "Besides, I keep a whole box of ammunition."

"You'll discover that I hid that box in your absence."

Isobel gaped. Before she could decide whether to be impressed or outraged, Riot pressed his advantage. "If you're determined to join the investigation, then you may as well make yourself useful."

"I'm always useful, Mr. Riot."

"That remains to be seen."

41

Ravenwood Agency

THE POLISHED PLAQUE ON the door was shaped like a raven in flight. Words were stamped on its breast: *Ravenwood's Detective Agency.* Isobel glanced at Riot and raised an amused brow. He adjusted his spectacles.

"I haven't been here yet."

"I thought these were your offices."

"I've been abroad. My partner used to conduct business from his home—it proved hazardous."

Before Isobel could interrogate him further, Riot opened the office door, and was immediately set upon by a furious little man.

"God damn you, A.J.!" Tim exploded, grabbing his lapels. "Where the devil have you been?" He looked on the verge of either throttling or hugging the younger man.

Riot briefly gripped Tim's shoulder, took a step back,

and primly straightened his coat.

"I was looking into a small matter." Tim's bright blue eyes focused on the young person lingering in the doorway, who by all accounts and purposes, looked like a teenage boy.

"Mr. Morgan," Riot introduced. "Percy Von Poppin, the head of Ravenwood Agency."

Isobel stepped in, whipped off her cap, and thrust out her hand. Tim shook it heartily, eyeing the faded bruises on her face. "Call me Tim, and I'm not the head," the wizened little man grumbled. "Those two fellows back there are Smith and Johnson."

Smith stepped forward, seized Isobel's hand, and shook it firmly. She made it a point to squeeze harder. Her hands had been roughed and strengthened by a childhood spent at sea.

"Good of you to return, Riot," Johnson called from his desk. He was a seedy looking bruiser with a drooping mustache and mutton chops. "Tim claims it's not permanent."

"It's not, I'm afraid."

Johnson smiled like a wolf. "I have five dollars riding on that very assumption."

"Not payable for another month," Tim protested. "Look, A.J., we need to talk." His eyes bounced from Isobel to Riot, and suggestively towards a side door in the small office. Isobel hooked her thumbs in her waistcoat, standing her ground.

"You found the *Magpie*," Riot surmised. "With a dead Captain Long on board. Shot in the head." Tim blinked, and Smith looked crestfallen.

Johnson slapped his knee in triumph. "You owe me a dollar, Smith."

"You heard." Tim frowned, dismayed.

Riot gestured towards his young companion. "You'll want to hear Mr. Morgan's version of events."

The men picked up their cigars and pipes, and filed through the side door that opened into a consultation room consisting of a polished table, chairs, and a window.

"Very professional, Tim," Riot commented, politely. "I don't doubt that you chose this location for its proximity to the Pinkerton offices."

"Annoyed the hell out of 'em," Tim cackled.

Isobel peered out the window, watching the bustling street far below, feigning disinterest with the men as they settled themselves in their chairs.

"Mr. Morgan will be joining our investigation," Riot said. All eyes focused on the newcomer by the window.

"That's right." Isobel turned, leaning on the sill. "As I should be. I'll not share what I have to let the lot of you get the reward money." She fished out a cigarette, struck a match across the wood with practiced ease, and brought the flame up to her face.

Riot was impressed. There wasn't a trace of woman in Isobel. She had the mannerisms of any young tramp. No doubt her position had been carefully chosen. Light from the window drew the eyes, casting her in shadow. And when she spoke, her voice was unaffected, deep without overcompensating. But then it came as little surprise. With nine brothers, mimicking an adolescent male would come naturally, especially for one who had spent a lifetime cross dressing and roving unsavory streets.

"As we agreed." Riot nodded to Isobel to continue.

"Capt'n Long hired me on, so I went to his boat. Two fellows jumped us, shot Long in the head, and sliced me good." She brandished her left forearm. The sleeve of her coat stretched over the padding of bandage.

Smith whistled low, and propped his boots on the table. The chair creaked in protest.

"The gunshots attracted attention," she continued. "The two bastards ran, and I also thought that wise. But before I hightailed it out of there, I pinched Long's belongings. He was dead broke."

Riot produced said belongings, setting a tarred billfold, battered compass, receipts, and five pasteboard cards on the table—the kind that prostitutes handed to prospective clients and paid boys a penny to pass out. Johnson lent forward to study the items.

"Since I recalled reading about a reward in the papers," Isobel continued, "and I didn't fancy going to the police, I sought out this here gentleman and we came to an agreement."

"Not to be too blunt," Tim interjected, glancing at Riot. "Was that wise?"

"I do believe it is, Tim," Riot countered. "Although I'd suggest keeping your billfolds close, gentlemen."

Isobel smirked.

"I already have to with the likes of Tim about," Johnson murmured around his cigar. He tapped the business cards. "Seems Long was an international sort. A Celestial harlot, Chileno, a bona fide golden goddess, and here's one for you, young Smith." He picked up the card and read it aloud. "Big Matilda. Three hundred pounds of black passion. Hours: All hours. Rates: 50c each: Three for one dollar. Hinckley Alley."

"Are you always so helpful, Johnson?" Isobel asked.

"More helpful than you've been so far," the bruiser challenged. "For a pickpocket between hay and grass who's taking a cut on our earnings, you're going to need more than some whore's business card."

"We do not accept reward money, Johnson," Riot reminded, cutting off Isobel's retort, which was sure to ruffle the detective's feathers. "We never have, and never will."

"We're off this case. How else do we expect to get paid?"

"You'll be paid as you always are," Tim said, thrusting his pipe stem at the man. "Now shut your trap before I have Riot swing that stick of his on your crown."

"He'll shut his trap just fine when he hears what I have to say," Isobel said, smugly. "Long was full as a tick when he hired me. Ran his mouth the entire time about two fellas by the name of Johnny Cox and Sam Quinn. I'll wager they're the same two that jumped us."

Johnson removed his cigar from his lips, Smith paled, and Tim whistled low.

"By your reactions, gentlemen," Riot observed. "I take it you are familiar with Cox and Quinn." He looked at each man in turn.

"A pair of curly wolves," Johnson huffed. "Not the kind of fellows you want to cross. You're damn lucky to be alive, boy."

"Do Quinn and Cox have a regular haunt?"

Johnson snorted. "Hiding out wherever you like between Pacific and Kearny. Boarding houses, cheap hotels, but like most flotsam, they all eventually wash up at the *Whale*, *Cowboy's Rest*, or the *Bull*."

Riot considered this. He pinned an ornate card with forget-me-nots around the border, and slid it closer, eyeing the advertisement: *Marabelle Gold, The Golden Goddess. All hours. Cowboy's Rest. $1 for your pleasure.* "They will likely stay away from the waterfront until the manhunt cools. And they've already visited *Cowboy's Rest*. I think they'll stay well away from that watering hole."

Captain Long had confessed that they'd picked up a girl at *Cowboy's Rest* that looked like Isobel. The golden goddess was likely the one. "That leaves the *Bull*. We'll need to enlist the police as witnesses during the interview. Is Quincy still a patrolman?"

"Detective now," answered Tim.

Riot arched an eyebrow. "Is he now? That is heartening."

"We'll need a police squad to drag them out of the *Bull*," Smith said. "I know an honest patrolman or two who might be willing."

"Have some faith, young Smith," Riot chided gently. "Our tactics are not as brutish as those of the police."

42

The Bull

RED LIGHTS GLOWED UNDER a sheen of luminous clouds. Heaven above and hell below. For all the damnations of preachers, the denizens of the underworld were a boisterous lot. The narrow lane was clogged with men, spilling out on the cobblestones, basking in debauchery.

Isobel wove her way through the throng, cap low, thumbs hooked on her lapels. She smiled to herself. A secret spot of mischief in the night. It surprised her—how easily Riot had agreed to her participation, as if he actually took her seriously.

The *Bull* was a three-story rookery that respectable whores avoided. A rippling bull, powerful, raging, and dominating decorated its brick front. It reminded her of Kingston, or how he fancied himself at any rate. In actuality, Isobel thought Kingston, and most men, more resembled yapping little dogs that were fond of rutting anything that remained still for more than ten seconds. The kind of pathetic nuisance that was best kicked out and ignored. Unfortunately, small dogs still had teeth.

Isobel strutted inside the *Bull*. A blast of piano keys filled the gaps between droning baritone voices. Tobacco moved in thick fog drifts over a sea of heads, masking the stench of stale beer and sweat. Rough men, sailors, thugs, and gentlemen perused the pretty waiter girls. The women's short red skirts, exposed garters, and snug waistcoats lured the men's eyes as much as their hands. And hopefully their dollars. After all, a pretty waiter girl was only as good as the money she earned for the dive.

As if nearly naked women roaming the floor weren't enough, a stage occupied the far end of the establishment, where a group of men jeered and hooted at a trio of women who compensated for their poor dance routine with high kicks and no bloomers.

One harried brunette set her sights on Isobel, who appeared to be easy prey. Ignoring the greedy paws of the patrons, the brunette sidled up to Isobel, wrapped an arm around her waist with one hand and presented a tray with the other. "A beer and cigar for a nickel."

Isobel paid her nickel, and made it a point to peruse the woman for show.

"Free samples on the floor, but you have to pay to play upstairs, honey." The waitress ran a hand down Isobel's waistcoat. When the waitress' touch glided over the youth's tightly bound breasts, her eyes flickered in surprise.

Isobel stuck the cigar between her lips and winked. For good measure, she sampled the brunette's flank with a sound slap. The woman laughed, deep and throaty, before sauntering over to a more promising customer.

Isobel glanced slyly at a gentleman in the corner. Whether affronted or shocked, she could not tell, but she definitely had his undivided attention. She brushed eyes with him. Riot's back was to the wall. And he looked a proper bruiser with bowler, cigar, and walking stick across his knees. Isobel decided Riot was a dangerous man of the worst sort: a distraction.

She promptly focused on her goal. Cox sat at a prime table in front of the stage, feasting on flesh with one eye while he pawed at the woman on his lap. Quinn sat off to the side in an alcove with a girl on either side. A cigar thrust upwards from his lips. Despite the company, his eyes roved the room with an air of alertness.

A brawl broke out in the center of the bar room. The crowd surged out, encircling the combatants. One good punch knocked the instigator flat. The crowd closed, and in short order the unconscious sailor's pockets were pilfered and he was dragged towards a back exit by an enterprising runner.

Unconscious sailors were worth fifty dollars to a needy captain.

Isobel tossed back her beer. It smelled like piss. Most of it dribbled down her chin and ended up on her waistcoat. She staggered forward, knocked into a pretty waiter girl, spilled more beer, and caught herself on Quinn's table, grinning like an idiot.

"Pardon me," she drawled to the Irishman.

The offended waitress cussed up a storm. Isobel emptied her pockets to appease the woman and Quinn's eyes narrowed on her tarred billfold. Recognition gleamed in the low light. His gaze strayed upwards, focusing on the face beneath the cap.

Isobel's eyes went wide. The recognition bleeding

through a drunken haze quickly blossomed into fear. She staggered backwards, bumping her way from patron to patron towards the back exit. Quinn stood, dislodging the women, who yelped in surprise.

"Cox!" Quinn shouted, slapping the ox's shoulder as he sprinted after the fleeing youth. The ox stood, then charged blindly through the crowd.

The two men pushed their way out the back, and into the night, emerging in a narrow alleyway. A fleeting shadow disappeared around a corner. Both men pursued. Their pounding footsteps bounced off the high brick walls.

They rounded the corner, and slowed, grinning from ear to ear. Brick walls rose all around. It was a dead end, full of refuse, and one trembling boy. Cox and Quinn walked slowly towards their prey.

"You're good and cornered, boy," Cox growled.

Three forms detached themselves from the shadows, one smaller, and two large. All three had shotguns.

"Not tonight fellows," said Tim.

Cox and Quinn reversed direction. Silver flashed in the dark, punching the ox's diaphragm. The air was expelled like a pair of bellows. Quinn reached for a revolver. The silver knob rapped his knuckles, and in a flurry of movement, struck knee cap and back, dropping the man to his side. Smith and Johnson rushed the ox, pinning him to the muck. Riot pressed the knob of his stick against Quinn's throat, and Tim retrieved the revolver, pointing it at his head.

"After what you did to that woman," Riot said with a voice that crawled under the men's skin, "I'd prefer you both dead. I urge you greatly, gentlemen, to fight and tempt your fate."

As much as Riot urged, neither man cared to test the

hovering shadow of death. In short order, and with no fuss, both men were trussed up securely.

Riot rested his stick on his shoulder. "And that, Smith, is how you lure rats out of their hole."

"Yes, sir." Smith grinned, hoisting Quinn upright. As Johnson manhandled Cox, Tim stood guard, and Riot moved beside Isobel.

"Well played, Miss Bel," he whispered beside her ear. His voice was low and deep, and plenty clear, but she found herself leaning near.

"To you as well, Mr. Riot. Nice and neat."

"The stage is surely missing an actress."

"I'm still young." She smiled. "You're a cool hand. Were you a gunfighter in another life?"

"A gambler in my youth."

"That explains it."

"What?"

"I noticed you were ambidextrous."

"A useful talent."

"In all things." The words were out of her mouth before she realized. She cleared her throat and changed the subject. "You'll take them to the station for questioning?" Her cheeks were warm.

Amusement flashed behind the glass, but his tone remained all business. "And hopefully persuade our despicable duo to confess."

"How will you do that?"

"I've a knack for persuasion."

"Of that I'm sure." Isobel glanced at Quinn and Cox. "One moment, Mr. Riot." She stepped in front of Quinn, and swung—a right hook to the jaw.

The man staggered, was held upright by Smith, and spat out a mouthful of blood, filling the alley with curses.

Isobel returned to Riot's side.

"Feel better?"

"I do," she replied, rubbing her knuckles.

"You best make yourself scarce, Miss Bel."

"You know where to find me, Mr. Riot."

Riot tipped his hat, eyes melting the shadow, and Isobel slipped into the night.

43

Five Card Draw

THE INTERROGATION ROOM IN the San Francisco police station was a depressing stone square, ten feet by ten feet, interrupted on one side by a barred door. A solid table was bolted to the floor. Two uncomfortable chairs faced each other across worn wood.

Sam Quinn was as subdued as the room. His discomfort was exacerbated by the handcuffs securing his wrists, which were wrenched behind his back. Leg irons weighed down his ankles.

A large patrolman stood by the door, blackjack poised to coax a confession. And a severe Captain Quincy stood to the side with another patrolman, who was ready with paper and pen.

Atticus Riot sat in the only other chair. His dark gaze was unwavering, appraising the man opposite. Quinn shifted beneath the penetrating eyes. He glanced from Riot to Quincy, and back again.

"You gonna stare at me all day?" Quinn asked in challenge.

"I certainly could, if you wish," Riot replied evenly.

"Like hell," Quinn spat. "Get on with the merry beating."

"There's no need to resort to brutality."

"Wasn't your opinion in the alley." Quinn looked to the Captain. "I didn't do a bloody thing. This dandy accosted me. Unprovoked."

Riot opened his coat, reached inside, and withdrew Captain Long's Tickler. He placed it on the table.

"Are you going to cut my throat?"

"Do you gamble, Mr. Quinn?" The question caught the criminal off guard.

"Course I do, nothing wrong with that."

"Dice, no doubt," Riot observed. "You strike me as man who doesn't like to wait for satisfaction."

"Life's too short."

Riot held up five business cards, arranging them like a poker hand. "There's a unique kind of satisfaction that can be had when a matter is drawn out." He placed the business cards on the table, face up. "I was never a faro man myself, but I did relish poker. It takes patience, all night if need be. After long hours spent at a poker table, a man can break down, lose his focus, start making mistakes, unconsciously throwing hands so he can bow out. I was never such a man, Mr. Quinn."

Quinn's eyes darted from the business cards and away, licking his lips.

"Keep in mind, we're playing five card draw, and the stakes are high," Riot smiled, "for you at any rate. Your neck is in the pot. And here are my first two cards." Riot pinned one card with his finger, sliding it across the table, right under Quinn's nose. "A knife, and a business card for Marabelle Gold, to be found at *Cowboy's Rest*. Now I happen to know the proprietress of that particular saloon. Cowboy Mag doesn't care for rough-handed patrons. After paying her a visit this afternoon, she said she'd be happy to place you and your friend with Marabelle."

"I didn't do a thing!" Quinn glanced at Captain Quincy. "He's trying for that reward money in the paper. Set to pin it on the first man he catches."

"Would you like to see my remaining cards?"

"Piss and wind."

"I'll take that as a yes." Riot nodded politely. "You haven't asked how I came by these items—a business card and a knife—because you recognized the young man in the alley tonight. He's my third card. And he's a witness to murder—the shooting of Captain W. Long. Unfortunately for you, Mr. Quinn, you were too late. Rum loosened Captain Long's tongue enough to confide in his young friend. He planned on selling you out for the reward money. I know about the wagon, the *Magpie* waiting at Whaler's Cove, and the sail that you wrapped Mrs. Kingston in when you abducted her from the ferry."

Quinn pressed his lips together. Jaw clenching, eyes burning a hole in Riot's forehead.

"As for my fourth card. I have yet another witness who saw you pay Old Sue to deliver that ransom letter to the Amsel residence. That witness placed you at the *Magpie*, the very boat where Mrs. Kingston's shoe was found in a crate, with a dead captain on her deck."

Quinn remained silent, paling with every word.

"The final card in my hand, Mr. Quinn, would be the

back alley physician, a Mr. Aubrey, who treated you and your friend Johnny Cox. It seems Mrs. Kingston put up quite a fight before she was driven overboard, likely with a bullet to speed her on her way."

Riot allowed the silence to deepen, for his words to take root and fester in Quinn's gut. "That's quite a hand," he said at length. "But I only need one card from you to lower the stakes. A wild card to save your neck. You see, I don't think you concocted this scheme by yourself."

Quinn's eye twitched, something shifted, a smugness in the corner of his lip.

"And you would be wrong in thinking your benefactor will bribe a jury on your behalf. He'll let you hang. A little fish like you, wiggling on the hook while the bigger swims safely away. A jury might look more favorably on you if you handed them that larger fish. At the very least, Mr. Quinn, you can hang knowing he has a noose around his neck too."

The words hung in the air between the men, growing heavy with hopelessness. Riot did not move. He simply waited, eyes locked on Quinn, who grew increasingly uncomfortable.

At last Quinn swallowed. "I don't know his name. We met in the *Cobweb Palace*. He gave us half up front. Told us where to find the girl, how to take her, what to write in the letter, when to kill her, and where to dump her, but the bitch went and got herself shot, and fell overboard. Probably washed out to sea by now."

"Did the man who hired you give his name?"

Quinn's lip twisted. "Course not."

"Description?"

"It was dark." He shrugged. "Had a sailor's look about him."

"A sailor?"

"That's right. A cap, scarf, collar turned up, but not the rough sort—not underneath the clothes. More like the yacht types down at the docks. He was a thin fellow. Real tall-like, and real pale. Sandy-haired and blue-eyed."

The blood froze in Riot's veins. And realization propelled him from the room.

44

Dear Brother Mine

WATER SLOSHED IN THE basin, swirling with the swells. Isobel dipped a cloth in hot water, squeezed out the excess, and washed the night's adventure from her skin. The stove warmed the cabin and oil lamps rocked on their tethers, throwing warm shadows over her body. She frowned at the angry yellow and black patches decorating her ribs. Cox's kick hadn't broken any bones, but he had left his boot print in her side.

Isobel wrung the washcloth, dipped, and repeated again until she fairly glowed. She ran a dry towel swiftly over her clipped hair, relishing its convenient length. It hadn't been difficult to shear the golden mass. After all, there was always a wig.

Her right hand hurt. The best kind of pain. The knuckles were bruised and swollen, and if given a chance, she'd punch Quinn a hundred times over.

Thoughts of Quinn turned to Riot—damn him. She had spent two hours pacing impatiently up and down the short cabin. Tried and failed to distract herself with a book, and finally decided to wash, concluding that he likely wouldn't return until morning with news of the interrogation. She had half a mind to rouse Riot from his bed and demand answers.

A soft knock against the hull froze her in place, raising her hackles. She reached for nightshirt and gun, ears straining. Cautious footsteps moved on deck. The storm covers were closed, keeping the light in and prying eyes out of the cabin. Senses straining, she followed the sound of footsteps moving above, towards the hatch.

Isobel cocked the revolver, pressed against the bulkhead, and stood her ground, aiming at the companionway ladder. The hatch opened, polished shoes gleamed in the night: long, thin, and expensive. A pinstriped trouser leg followed, and then a face. The man's mouth gaped, and bright blue eyes went wide with shock.

Isobel narrowed her eyes. "Curtis," she said his name like a vile oath. Disappointment, surprise, and dread warred in her voice.

"Isobel!" Curtis staggered down the ladder and sat heavily on the first rung. She eased the hammer down, and stood frowning at her older brother.

"You're alive," he gasped.

"No, I'm a ghost, Curtis." Conscious of her thin night shirt and damp skin, she set the gun down on the table, moved her book aside on the berth, and retrieved a blanket, wrapping it around her shoulders. "Next time you board a boat in the middle of the night, I'd suggest a courteous, 'ahoy there', brother. I nearly shot you. How did you find me?"

"I wondered why Mr. Riot asked after Lotario, so I called on our brother. When the *Pagan Lady* wasn't in her berth, I thought it was stolen and decided to track it down." Curtis moved into the cabin. "Everyone thinks you're dead."

"And I aim to keep it that way."

"So do I, little sister." Curtis picked up her revolver with his left hand, slipped it into his pocket, and produced one of his own with his right. The hammer was already cocked, and the barrel was leveled at her heart.

Isobel blinked. Words stuck in her throat, breath turned stale, and her mind emptied. The oil lamp swayed between brother and sister. Shock numbed her, and the boat rocked with a dreamlike consistency.

"Sit," Curtis ordered.

Isobel swallowed, and found her voice. "I'd rather not."

"Always pig-headed. You won't even die quietly." The words plunged into her heart, and twisted.

"It was you," she breathed. "You hired Cox and Quinn. *Why?*" The question was a plea, not for her life but for the betrayal.

"You have caused me a great deal of trouble over the years," he explained with a voice of reason. "When Kingston took an interest in you, I began to wonder why a man in his position would want my loud-mouthed, slip-of-an-annoying sister."

"Most men like a big mouth," she replied cheekily.

"And vulgar," Curtis hissed, flushing with anger. The weapon in his hand trembled.

"You knew what Kingston was doing all along, didn't you?"

"Of course I did. Kingston and I move in the same circles. How do you think I was able to silence the press on your behalf?"

"You were content to stand aside while our family's livelihood was sabotaged," Isobel surmised. "That is, until you learned that mother's property was valuable."

"So you know?"

"Isn't it obvious?" To Riot at any rate, she added silently. "Were you planning on murdering mother and father after disposing of your inconvenient sister?"

"Nothing so diabolical. I'm a patient man. After all I've done for you, it will be an easy matter to persuade mother to pass her holdings on to my own daughter."

"I don't think you're as patient as you believe, Curtis." The room was cold, and so dreadfully still. "I think you will arrange an early death for our dear parents. Something beneficial, like you did with the young woman who took my place in death. So what was it that was in your way: the railway line or the shrimping village?"

"How truly naive," he said, disappointed. "You don't see it, do you? I'm an Engineer, sister, in more ways than one. Exactly like Kingston, but not near so clumsy. We are not so petty and narrow-sighted as that. There are powerful men in the shadows—men who can accomplish anything."

Isobel smirked. "They can't seem to kill one slip of a girl."

"That will change shortly."

"All for the money, Curtis?"

"No, little sister." He smiled, slowly backing into the galley. "I'm tired of silencing your scandals, but mostly—you've always annoyed the hell out of me." With his left hand, he opened a storage door in the galley, unscrewed the cap to the paraffin stores, and knocked the container on the floor. Threatening fumes clogged the cabin.

Isobel snorted derisively. "You can't even shoot me yourself?"

"Less evidence."

"No," she argued. "It's the coward's way."

Curtis stepped on the first rung, fishing in his pocket for a lighter.

"You are forgetting one very important detail, brother."

"Doubtful." He flipped open the top.

"I'm as mad as a hatter." Isobel dropped her blanket, grabbed the book off the berth and swung *The Adventures of Sherlock Holmes* at the oil lamp. Glass, oil, and flame exploded, spraying the galley. A shot fired, going wide. Flame sparked, caught, and the cabin was engulfed.

Curtis stumbled up the companionway, batting at his burning coat. Isobel grabbed the heavy berth mat, threw it on the burning paraffin, and sprinted after. Flames licked at her wet skin.

The hatch swung towards her, and she thrust her book between door and post. She moved up the ladder. Smoke chased her, swarming through the crack. Curtis slammed the hatch down again, and she reeled back, ducking, coughing, eyes burning. The hatch lifted, and she threw her shoulder against the wood, desperate to dislodge Curtis' weight; desperate for air.

A gunshot ripped through her panic. The hatch relented, and she burst into cool air, dazed and staggering. A hand seized her throat, metal pressed into her temple, and blood filled her senses.

Curtis was wheezing with pain. And, damn it, her night shirt was on fire.

"Stay where you are, Mr. Riot!" Curtis' rasp grated on

her ears. Isobel glimpsed movement through a scupper. Curtis compensated for Riot's flanking attempt, wielding her like a shield. She braced her foot on the coaming, and pushed off, throwing her weight fully against her larger brother. He stumbled backwards, and hit the rail.

Isobel slipped her hand in his coat pocket, found the trigger to her Colt, and squeezed. There was no sound. Time turned lazy. And the moon was impossibly bright. Curtis jerked, falling backwards, his finger spasmed, and another shot pierced the night.

Sister and brother plunged overboard.

45

Death's Final Gift

RIOT AND TIM CLIMBED over the rail, and raced to the other side of the deck. A pale cloud billowed under the water, cloth swaying like kelp. Two shadows surfaced. Isobel clutched her limp brother, laboring to keep him afloat. He made unnatural sounds in the dark—a gurgle and gasp, choking on his own blood.

Isobel's cry turned watery as she bobbed back under the icy black. Riot bent over the rail, reaching for Isobel. His fingers found fabric and he tugged her against the hull.

"Take Curtis," she spluttered.

Together, Tim and Riot pulled the man up and over. Curtis was dead when he hit the deck.

"There's a fire, Tim," Riot reminded, reaching for Isobel again. Riot hooked his hands under her arms, and Tim sprang towards the cabin. She slid over the rail to land on deck, limp as a fish.

"Are you all right?" Riot's hands roved over her face, head, and body, searching for injury. However, her wounds were deeper than any bullet. She pushed Riot away, and fell on Curtis, probing for a pulse with trembling fingers.

"Damn you," she coughed, and with more strength repeated the sentiment, pounding her fist against his chest. "Damn you!" The words wrenched from her throat, fist struck again, and a single sob shook her body. "You greedy, yellow-bellied bastard!" Rage was set to descend for a third time, but Riot grabbed her wrist, halting the blow.

"Bel," he said, softly.

"Damn him," she repeated, hoarsely.

"I think he's good and damned." Riot gently pulled her away. For a moment, she resisted, but he persisted and she came, burying her grief in his arms. A storm shook her body, and Riot tightened his hold, pressing her head to his shoulder.

There was nothing to say. But there was something to do. Riot pulled back, long enough to remove his coat. He draped it over her shoulders and helped her stand.

Gunshots and smoke had attracted attention. Bullseye lanterns probed the boat from shore.

"Tim will take you somewhere safe."

"I'm fine. Leave me be." She shook off his hands, huddling beneath his coat.

"Look at me, Bel," Riot ordered, gripping her arms. "The police are coming. Unless you want to return to this side of the veil, I suggest you go with Tim. I'll remain and make up a suitable story, but I can't do that if you're here."

"Yes," she murmured. "Yes, of course."

As if summoned, Tim appeared, popping his head out of the hatch. "The fire is contained. I spent a month in a fire brigade. There's no damage that can't be repaired." The older man eyed the shivering person in Riot's coat, and then blinked in shock. Face and hair named the young person as Mr. Morgan, but the body beneath the wet and clinging nightshirt was most decidedly female.

"This is Mrs. Kingston, Tim." Riot drew her towards their dinghy. "Call her Bel, and not a word to anyone. Take her to the turret room and see to her needs. I'll handle the police."

Tim hopped into the dinghy, and Riot handed Isobel down to the attentive man. She complied without protest, which worried Riot no end.

"Did you know, Miss Bel," Tim said, gripping the oars, "I've spent the occasional night as a runner. This is just like the good ol' days."

The voice and dinghy faded into the night, leaving Riot with a third corpse, and his heart reaching towards a woman who, by all accounts, should be dead.

46

The Calm

SATURDAY, JANUARY 6, 1900

THE LAMPS WERE DORMANT, but the hearth glowed, throwing shadows against crates. Riot paused in the doorway, scanning the dim room. Wearily, he hung his bowler on its hook, unbuckled his holster, rolled the straps around the leather, and set it on the small table by the doorway.

The void against his ribs was a relief. He had aimed to stop, not to kill. One bullet to Curtis Amsel's shoulder. However, in retrospect, he wished he had aimed for his head. At least then Isobel's fury would be with him, and not with herself. It would have removed the burden of guilt. No one should have to shoot their own blood.

Riot glanced towards the bed, tucked between draped furniture and crates. The covers were undisturbed. His gaze was pulled to the fire, and then to the back of Raven-wood's throne-like armchair. He sensed her there.

A tray of food, untouched, sat on the table between chairs. The tea had long gone cold. He moved into the room, passing the armchair with a sparing glance, on his way to a crate. Isobel looked fragile and small in Raven-wood's chair. Her legs were drawn up, tucked under a blanket that reached her chin. She stared into the fire, eyes shining gold in the light.

Riot removed the lid to one crate, then another, look-ing for something in particular. When he did not find it in either, he turned to a piece of draped furniture, and nearly kicked himself. Nothing had been touched, not really. He pulled off a drape to reveal a sideboard, opened it and plucked a bottle from its depths.

Her eyes flicked away from the fire, watching his movements as he picked up the teacup, flung its cold con-tents into the fire, and filled it to the brim with Southern Comfort. She took his offer, and he sat opposite.

"Your coat is dry," she said after a long swallow. Riot nodded. Failing to find a second cup, he drank from the bottle. Smooth heat washed away the night.

"Did Tim see to your arm?" In answer, she raised her left forearm, brandishing a clean, dry bandage. Riot took another swig, and Isobel emptied her own cup. He filled it again. When her second cup was empty, she retreated beneath her blanket, resting her cheek against the chair, eyes on the flames.

"Everything is settled," he said, breaching the silence. "Quinn confessed at the station, leading me to Curtis. I told the police that he was trying to make his escape on his brother's yacht. Curtis wouldn't come quietly, so I shot him in the shoulder, he fell back, and the revolver in his pocket discharged when he reached for it. Since his own weapon is at the bottom of the bay, the police believed my version of events."

"You were right," she admitted. "Kingston and Curtis were after my inheritance."

"I wish I wasn't."

"I wanted it to be Kingston."

"He's committed his share of crimes."

"And so have I," she whispered. "I've killed my brother. Even if I manage to hang Kingston, I can't ever face my parents."

"Your brother was an ass," Riot stated bluntly.

She blinked. "How crude, Mr. Riot."

"Are we back to formalities, Miss Bel?"

"Not tonight." The edge of her lip lifted. "But you're right, Curtis was always an ass. I reckon I gave him good reason."

"For attempted murder? For hiring a pair of dimwitted cutthroats who left a long trail of blood in their wake?" Riot clucked his tongue. "Nothing excuses that."

"You're not going to let me wallow in my guilt, are you?"

"If you hadn't shot Curtis, I would have."

"I can't say I pulled the trigger for the right reason," Isobel admitted. "If Curtis had lived, he would have told everyone that I was still among the living. And I couldn't bear that."

Riot studied her in the firelight. The words were honest, her defenses shredded by despair. Isobel Saavedra Amsel had already lived more than most would ever live in twenty years. And yet, she was still young and full of doubt —no matter how much she tried to conceal her inexperience. As such, Riot took his time in answering, choosing his words with the utmost care.

"I've killed more than my fair share of men, Bel. No matter the reason, I can't say a single one was for the right reason—only necessary."

The coals shifted. Isobel met his gaze, unflinching and open. Finally, she nodded once. She reached for the bottle, ignored the teacup, and took a long swallow.

"Curtis' death will break my parents. He's always been their golden boy."

"In this case, concealing the truth of the matter would have roused suspicion."

"I know," she sighed.

"There's always divorce."

"We've been through this," she said, wearily. "If I reappear now, after Curtis' involvement has come to light, Kingston would very likely turn the tables and claim it was a conspiracy to steal his money—especially if it came out that I sent the ransom letters to the newspapers."

"I blamed those on Curtis, too."

"Did you? How thoughtful," she said with warmth. "Regardless, Kingston has too much on me. He owns too many people. I can accomplish more by continuing the ruse."

"*I must be cruel only to be kind,*" Riot quoted under his breath.

Isobel's eyes flashed, and she finished the quote, "*Thus bad begins and worse remains behind.*"

Riot smiled, tilting his head. "I wouldn't be so sure about that, Miss Bel. You're not entirely without friends anymore."

"You're a dangerous man, Mr. Riot."

"Of the best sort."

The Bone Orchard

SATURDAY, JANUARY 13, 1900

AS FAR AS FUNERALS went, Isobel Kingston's was an impressive affair, spawning a long line of landaus and phaetons. All of society was garbed in beautiful death.

The tailors rejoiced. The undertaker's wife nearly fainted with glee, and the stonemason who was commissioned to build her eternal resting place could have retired if he'd so desired. Even the sun came out to grace the affair.

Isobel leaned against a tombstone, watching her funeral from afar. Her guests were perched around a pillared mausoleum like a murder of crows. She began to wonder if Alex Kingston had been fond of her after all.

All seven remaining brothers, Hop, the household staff,

and her mother and father were miserably gathered. If she were going to cause her family grief, she may as well have the decency to endure theirs—as painful as it was to witness.

Smoke trailed from a cigarette between her lips. She removed it, flicking the ashes on Zephaniah Ravenwood's grave. Her eyes kept drifting to a certain man among the crows. Atticus James Riot wore a top hat well. Not many men did. Kingston looked like a bull stuffed into a penguin suit. And as for her father and brothers—she sorely wanted to look away.

"This too shall pass," she murmured to the man beneath the earth. The reminder didn't help. At some point, she realized her cheeks were wet. It seemed too much effort to wipe away her tears, so she let them bleed into the earth. Only ghosts were there to witness her grief.

Slowly, one by one, individuals broke away, each placing a rose at the foot of her stony mansion before leaving. All save Riot.

The crowd thinned, then dwindled, leaving her family. While the men waited, her mother disappeared inside the mausoleum.

When her mother finally emerged, bent and old, Isobel wished herself dead. Eventually, even her family disappeared, leaving her alone in the bone orchard with its dead.

Without warning, a bespectacled gentleman appeared, stepping from behind a gravestone. She used her sleeve to scrub away tears. At the sight of the gravestone supporting her back, the man paused and paled.

"I hope you don't mind that your friend kept me company," she sniffled. Riot blinked as if she were speaking a foreign tongue.

"Yes." His throat was raw, and he coughed, clearing away pain. "I mean no, not at all. Ravenwood always made for intolerable company." He drifted closer, as if pulled against his will.

"So do I."

At her words, Riot relaxed, planting his stick in the ground and resting his hands on the knob. Isobel stood, and dusted off her trousers. She eyed him from head to toe, and then back up again.

"You look a proper dandy, Mr. Riot."

There was no denying it. Riot tucked his stick under his arm, swept off his top hat and bowed in the courtliest of manners. Thick raven hair gleamed in the sunlight. A red rose appeared in his hand. And Isobel laughed, deep from her belly, plucking it from his hand.

"I feel underdressed, or do you make a habit of offering roses to tramps?"

Riot eyed her male attire. "A habit I'll be sure to take up."

Isobel buried her nose in the rose, hiding her smile. "This is the loveliest funeral gift I've ever received, Mr. Riot."

"I half expected you to be a pirate at your own funeral," he admitted.

"I've always been more of a Huckleberry than a Tom."

"A new *nom de plume* for you?"

"There's a sure way to attract attention."

"That reminds me." Riot reached beneath his coat and brought out his billfold. "Mr. Morgan's reward money. See that he gets it, will you?"

Isobel looked at the money as if it were a viper in his hand. "Give it to Marabelle's family." She waved dismissively.

"I spoke with Mag, the proprietress of *Cowboy's Rest* where Marabelle kept a room. Mag said her father started pimping her out when she was twelve. She has no other family."

"Oh."

"At least Marabelle has a fine resting place." Riot glanced towards the marble mausoleum.

"Marabelle's in there?" Isobel asked in surprise.

"It'd be a shame to waste such a fine burial chamber," Riot stated cryptically.

Isobel narrowed her eyes. "You bribed the undertaker, didn't you?"

"Am I so transparent?"

"Only to me." Their eyes locked. "May I ask a favor of you, Mr. Riot?"

"Ask, Miss Bel."

"Would you take that reward money and purchase the *Pagan Lady* from my brother?"

Riot raised his brows in surprise. He tucked the reward away, and adjusted his spectacles, as if the angle were wrong and a new one would help make sense of her request.

"I—" he hesitated, and then simply fell silent.

Isobel frowned at his uncharacteristic stumble. His eyes flickered to a point over her shoulder, and she followed his gaze to Ravenwood's tombstone.

"Curtis is dead, Mr. Riot," she reminded, facing him square.

"I do recall, Miss Bel. It's only—I think the boat an ill place to live."

"I take my memories with me, wherever I go. If I run from that boat, then Curtis and I will never make peace."

Riot stared at the young woman. Her words sliced to

the bone, and he found he had none left of his own. Isobel considered him for a long moment. She stepped closer, brushing an invisible speck off his shoulder. His breath was shallow and his dark eyes were wide.

Slowly, she raised her hand to the white wing above his temple, slashing through his jet hair. The skin beneath the white was smooth and jagged all at once. A deep rut in his scalp. His breath caught.

"I thought so," she whispered, probing the old wound with her fingertips. "Wounds to the head might heal, but the hair often grows back differently. It was a bullet, wasn't it?"

Riot nodded once, closing his eyes against a barrage of memory. He tilted his head slightly, pressing against her fingertips. Her touch tethered him to the present.

"It has to do with your partner's death?" Again, he nodded. "I remember reading about his murder in the newspapers. A gruesome business."

"It was," he rasped in pain. "I found him in pieces."

"Is that what the R.I.P stands for: Rest in Pieces?"

Riot frowned.

"Sorry." Isobel winced, removing her hand. "My mouth gets away with my thoughts."

"I don't think I've ever met anyone quite like you, Miss Bel."

"You don't think?"

"Not that I recall."

"Are women of my kind that forgettable?"

"Quite the opposite."

"Then I'm sure you'd remember."

"I stand corrected," he whispered. "I can say with absolute certainty that I have *never* met anyone like you."

"Good." She smiled. "I'd be dreadfully jealous otherwise."

"Would you?"

"We'll never know. There's only one of me."

"I'm not sure the world could tolerate two."

"It doesn't even have to tolerate one anymore. I'm dead. And I feel wonderful." She turned back to Raven-wood's grave.

"I wish I could say the same of myself," Riot murmured at her shoulder. Isobel glanced at him, hesitated, and then reached into her pocket.

"Obviously, you're not a sailor."

"Why do you say that?" he asked, curious.

"Every sailor worth his salt learns one very important lesson: the sea eventually swallows everyone. A sailor must make his peace or he'll never come home."

Isobel pressed something cool and hard against his palm, closing his fingers around the object. She squeezed his hand once, and abruptly stepped back, hurrying off without another word.

Riot watched her disappear, feeling as though a part of him had left. He uncurled his fingers. A cartridge sat in his palm. Riot stared uncomprehendingly at the brass cylinder. When realization finally dawned, he smiled, closing his fist protectively around the offering of trust. Bel was right, she only needed one.

For the very first time since Zephaniah Ravenwood's murder, Riot found the courage to face his partner's grave.

*"For last year's words belong to last year's language
And next year's words await another voice.
And to make an end is to make a beginning."*
—*T.S. Eliot*

If you enjoyed FROM THE ASHES and would like to see more of Bel and Riot, please consider leaving a review on various online book sites. Your feedback can open doors that otherwise remain firmly closed for Indie authors.

Historical Afterword

THERE ARE A NUMBER of references to historical figures and places in this book: Cowboy Mag, Johnny McNear, Father Caraher, The Lively Flea, Big Matilda (that was a real business card), and many others.

Historical references for these colorful figures are few and far between. While I attempted to be as accurate as possible, I wasn't always able to pinpoint exact dates. Since this is a work of fiction, I tossed my characters into a temporal anomaly, and this may have caused alterations to the Space Time Continuum.

✛

The following is an actual ransom note:

"You wil have to pay us before you git him from us, and pay us a big cent to if you put the cops hunting for him you is only defeegin yu own end."

It was written in 1874 and was the first ransom note sent in America. The case involved the abduction of a little boy, Charley Ross.

✜

Truth is often stranger than fiction. During my research of San Francisco's Barbary Coast and the surrounding areas, I uncovered a gold mine of the truly bizarre. (Anyone who has lived in or near San Francisco will know that the bizarre is still alive and thriving.)

Isobel's early life is based loosely on Aimée Crocker, sometimes known as Princess Aimée Crocker-Ashe-Gillig-Gourand-Miskinoff-Galitzine, who was an heiress to a fortune, roamed the docks as a child, was sent to a Dresden finishing school, had her chaperone ditch her, and then proceeded to roam Europe with a group of friends—unchaperoned. And yes, she did stop in the middle of an aisle to light up a cigarette as a flower girl. However, where Aimée had a passion for men, Isobel has a passion for detective work.

Regardless, there are numerous women throughout San Francisco's history who did whatever they pleased. And countless instances of women masquerading as men.

✜

For anyone interested in this time period and setting, the book '*The Barbary Coast: An informal History of the San Francisco Underworld*' by Herbert Asbury is a fascinating read.

Acknowledgments

It's amazing what can spark an idea. A gravestone in England's Highgate Cemetery gave birth to Zephaniah Ravenwood (what a cool name I thought) and his partner Atticus James Riot. And then what was supposed to be a short story for a mystery contest turned into a full fledged novel, and one day, into a series.

But I certainly couldn't have finished this book alone. And I didn't. I am very fortunate to have a great team of people who are all possessed of sharper eyes than me.

A huge thanks to my editors Tom Welch and Merrily Taylor who never fail to attack my manuscripts with a relish. I take full responsibility for any grammar errors, since I probably 're-corrected' something that was already corrected.

Annelie Wendeberg and I have developed a habit of bludgeoning each other over the head with our first draft edits. I've had innumerable arguments with her, although she's never present, and only after I've exhausted myself, I discover (once again) that she was right. I value her blunt criticism immensely and I'd like to think she has the same sort of mental arguments with me whenever I hand her back an edited manuscript.

To Alice Wright, who has a keen eye for detail. She never fails to push me to do better. I count on her critical eye, blunt honesty, and live for her 'well done'. Thank you so very much!

A huge thanks to the very kind folks at www.sailnet.com. Thanks for being patient with this dirt dweller who was very confused by a number of nautical terms. Hopefully, I got my aft and stern; cutter vs sloop; gaff-rails and saloons all in order.

To Paula and Ginny who have endured countless cover concepts. Thank you for advising and helping me tweak, and then not getting upset when I throw everything out the window and start over again.

And thank you Janis McDermott. Much to my delight, she eagerly volunteered her sharp eyes. And even better, she wants to keep me! A writer can never have too many critical beta-readers.

My family deserves more credit than I can give in a few words. Nonetheless, thank you for putting up with months of absentmindedness, distraction, and then being understanding enough to let me do it all over again when I plunge into the next book.

Finally, thank you to my readers. You make the months of solitary work worth it.

About the Author

Sabrina lives in perpetual fog and sunshine with a rock troll and two crazy imps. She spent her youth trailing after insanity, jumping off bridges, climbing towers, and riding down waterfalls in barrels. After spending fifteen years wrestling giant hounds and battling pint-sized tigers, she now travels everywhere via watery portals leading to anywhere.

CPSIA information can be obtained
at www.ICGtesting.com
Printed in the USA
FSHW020509301019
63555FS